the
TRUTH
TRACKERS
CHARLES
MILLS

REVIEW AND HERALD® PUBLISHING ASSOCIATION
HAGERSTOWN, MD 21740

The author assumes full responsibility for the accuracy of
all facts and quotations as cited in this book.

This book was
Edited by Randy Fishell
Cover/interior design by Trent Truman
Cover art by Mark Bender
Electronic makeup by Shirley M. Bolivar
Typeset: 11/15 Optima

PRINTED IN U.S.A.

05 04 03 02 01   5 4 3 2 1

R&H Cataloging Service
Mills, Charles Henning, 1950-
    The truth trackers.

    1. Title.

        813.54

ISBN 0-8280-1462-0

Dorinda,

I love you—

and that's the truth!

OTHER BOOKS
BY CHARLES H. MILLS:

PROFESSOR APPLEBY AND MAGGIE B SERIES:
Adventure Stories From the Bible
Amazing Stories From the Bible
Heroic Stories From the Bible
Love Stories From the Bible
Miracle Stories From the Bible
Mysterious Stories From the Bible

SHADOW CREEK RANCH SERIES:
Escape to Shadow Creek Ranch
Mystery in the Attic
Secret of Squaw Rock
Treasure of the Merrilee
Whispers in the Wind
Heart of the Warrior
River of Fear
Danger in the Depths
A Cry at Midnight
Attack of the Angry Legend
Stranger in the Shadows
Planet of Joy

Eyes of the Crocodile
Bible-Based Answers to Questions Kids Ask
Echoing God's Love
My Talents for Jesus/When I Grow Up (Pacific Press)
Secrets From the Treasure Chest
The Touch of the Master's Hand

CONTENTS

CHAPTER 01

BIG CITY BLUES

Tony Parks stood beside the big yellow farmhouse, squinting into the late-afternoon haze. Beyond the barn he could make out the shadowy forms of the milk cows lumbering down from the south pasture, eager to eat the fresh hay scattered by the water trough.

In his hands Tony held a small metal box with toggle switches, buttons, and a bright screen. Tiny colorful lights flickered across the face of the device. Tony gazed at the beautiful scene around him.

Suddenly someone called his name, the summons echoing from the direction of the barn.

"It's open," the boy declared, not taking his eyes from the distant animals.

A door appeared at the base of the barn, and a girl stepped through it. She stood for a long moment, enjoying the peaceful surroundings, then spoke softly. "I remember," she said. "It was just like this."

Tony frowned as a sigh escaped his lips. "No, Tie Li," he countered. "It was more beautiful."

Suddenly the cows vanished, leaving the pasture

empty. The boy pressed a button on the device, and the house and barn dissolved into empty space. Then he lifted the box to his lips and ordered, "SIMON, clear buffers and reset VR phase receptors. Stand by with 20 percent spin. Set default condition."

In a flash all remnants of the scene disappeared, throwing the area into total darkness. Then lights flickered on overhead.

Tie Li looked across the empty expanse that was now the large, trash-littered, abandoned storage area of an old warehouse. She sighed. "I liked how it looked before."

"Yeah," Tony agreed, entering a small office tucked inside a nearby wall. "Think I have it just about right. SIMON processed those photographs I scanned last night and integrated the data nicely. I've gotta get more memory chips, though. Reproducing cows in virtual reality is one thing. Reproducing moving cows is a whole new ball game."

Tie Lie blinked. "Do cows play ball?"

"Don't start with me, little sister," Tony warned with a grin. "You know what I mean. Three years ago maybe I'd have to explain. But you're 12 now and understand English better than I do."

The girl tossed back long strands of jet-black hair and giggled. "You teached me good," she teased.

"Taught. *Taught!*" Tony said, laughing.

The two siblings chuckled over their private joke. It felt good to laugh, even over something as silly as Tie Li's use of bad grammar, a habit she'd overcome completely.

Three years before no one was laughing when the

Parks family adopted a frail, frightened orphan left homeless by a war raging in a faraway country. Tie Li had changed their lives with her gentle innocence. Now she was a confident 12-year-old who spoke in clear, precise phrases built on perfect grammar.

Tony slumped onto a bent metal chair. "It's not the same," he said with a sigh.

Tie Li shook her head slowly. "No, Tony, it's not. But I like to remember with you. It makes me happy inside."

"I'll never forget how that storm took everything," the boy recalled. "Our house. Our barn. *Voyager.** Everything."

"No," Tie Li countered. "It didn't take us. We're still here."

Tony stood and walked to a window. Pulling back a faded curtain, he allowed sunlight to flood the little office with streams of dusty brilliance. Outside, tall buildings rose skyward, etching themselves into the cold winter blue. "I hate the city," he said. "It's dirty. It's noisy. And I can't watch the cows anymore."

Tie Li studied the silhouette of her 14-year-old brother. His usually energetic shoulders sagged under the weight of disappointment. The baseball cap that used to rest proudly atop his thatch of blond hair sat low over his eyes, as if he were trying to hide from something.

At one time he'd been happy and alive, wandering flowering fields with her, showing her the secrets of nature, reveling in the freedom of open spaces and clean, country air.

But a devastating tornado had ripped through the farm, and the family had moved to Chicago. There Mr. Parks had accepted a position in a mid-sized company as an agricultural consultant. Tony had changed after the move. It seemed that the storm had sucked up his spirit along with the farm, leaving a sad, lonely shell behind–a shell that before had encased a genius.

"How do you do that? How does that computer make this warehouse look like our old farm?" the girl asked, trying to sound enthusiastic.

The boy shook his head. "You wouldn't understand, Tie Li."

"Yes, I would." The young girl had learned that the only time her brother seemed at all interested in life these days was when he was talking computers. "Is it magic?" she asked.

Tony chuckled. "No. It's not magic. It's called 'virtual reality.'" He motioned toward a large metal case sitting in one corner of the office. "I feed information into that main processor, and it creates images based on the data by painting an electronic picture in three dimensions using those projectors in the rafters." Tie Li saw several odd-shaped devices hanging above the warehouse floor. "It's no big deal. The military has been doing VR experiments for years. Now a lot of people are getting into it."

"So, you can make any place you want?" the girl pressed.

"Not 'make' for real," Tony explained, "but simulate. Kinda make a pretend version that seems really real. And yes, SIMON and I can simulate a lot of places, as long as I've got enough data—and memory chips."

"And you call the processor SIMON after our friend in Florida?"

Tony nodded his head as the hint of a grin creased his young face. "Like all computers, this one's touchy and very unpredictable, just like Simon Gorby was when we took him on Voyager expeditions. The word also means Standard Information Monitor. SIMON is easier to say."

"Tell me more about how it works." Tie Li looked at her brother.

"Well, SIMON is voice-responsive."

"What does that mean?" Tie Li asked.

"It means I don't always have to enter information on the keyboard, or receive it on-screen," Tony patiently explained. "I can interact with SIMON by speaking."

"Does that make SIMON a human being?" Tie Li wondered aloud.

"No," her brother said, chuckling. "Just like any computer, SIMON only spits out information based on what I've fed in. He's still very much a machine."

Suddenly Tony paused, eyeing his younger sister with suspicion. "Wait a minute. You're not just trying to cheer me up by asking a bunch of computer questions, are you?"

The girl gasped. "Who, me? No. I'm really interested. Where else could I learn about VP?"

"VR."

"Yes, that too."

Tony burst out laughing. "Tie Li, get outta here! I've gotta pack this stuff up and return it to Dad's office in case Mr. Lester needs his spare server."

Tie Li nodded. "OK. I'll see you back at the apartment. Don't be late for supper. Mom and I are making fake meatballs with gravy. Might even get some rocky road ice cream at the market. How's that sound?"

"Sounds like you're still trying to cheer me up."

"Hey," the girl said, laughing, "you're not the only person who likes to help people. After all, you built *Voyager* for me. The least I can do is make you some meatballs."

Tony lifted his hands. "OK. I'm all warm and fuzzy inside now." He paused. "Thanks, little sister. You're the best."

"I know," she giggled. "I had a good teacher."

With that, Tie Li left the warehouse through the same door she'd entered earlier.

Tony glanced at the device resting on the table beside him. "SIMON," he called.

The word activated two quick beeps from the small unit as a "ready" light flickered on. Then a metallic voice responded, "SIMON standing by."

Tony spoke a standard question into the device's microphone. "Give data report on how much memory is needed for full-effects simulation."

After a pause, the computer responded, "Simulation played at . . . fifty-seven point four-two percent of needed power. For full effects, resources needed are . . . nine point six-eight gigabytes of system memory . . . and three additional in-line processors."

Tony moaned. Ten gigabytes of memory and three more processors! Where was he going to find that kind of computing power?

He flipped a switch on the device and gathered up his equipment. Stacking everything on a low four-wheel cart, he hurried away, leaving the warehouse empty and dark.

Tony didn't see the hand that snatched the keyboard off the cart. One moment it was there, lying safely across the processor and a 3-D projector. The next moment it was gone.

"Hey!" he shouted, causing heads to turn in his direction. "Hey! Someone stole my keyboard!"

The people on the sidewalk looked at each other suspiciously, then continued on their way.

"Didn't anyone see anything?" Tony called to the passing mass of men and women.

Then his eye caught a split-second glimpse of someone rushing around the corner at the busy intersection. Was that a keyboard the person was carrying?

Tony jammed his cart behind a newsstand and hollered at the proprietor. "Mr. Pierce, watch this for me. I'll be right back." A large man wearing a canvas apron smeared with decades of newsprint ink waved the afternoon edition over his head.

"Sure thing, Tony. Go catch the bum!"

In seconds Tony ran around the corner, bouncing off pedestrians, careening between sidewalk displays, and jumping over boxes being unloaded from a delivery truck. He strained to keep the fleeing felon in sight.

Suddenly the individual turned and dived into an alley. Tony accelerated his pace, flashing past flinching people who grabbed their bags protectively.

"Sorry," Tony called back over his shoulder.

Into the alley he turned, rounding the next corner to the right and then another to the left. He sped along, leaping over dented trash cans and scattered piles of dank-smelling litter.

Seeing a dead end, closed off completely by a tall brick wall, Tony skidded to a halt, panting for breath. He glanced around, ready to pounce on the thief he knew must be hiding nearby.

"Come on out!" he called angrily between gasps. "I know you're back there somewhere, and you've got my keyboard!"

He saw a slight movement behind a pile of discarded cardboard boxes.

"So, are you going to give it back, or do I come after you?"

"You look as dangerous as a puppy," a young-sounding voice responded from behind the heap of trash.

Tony blinked. "Hey, I caught you, didn't I? Are you going to give me my keyboard? It doesn't even belong to me. It's from my dad's company, and if I don't return it, I'm in big trouble."

"What is it worth to you?"

"Why, you—" Tony lunged toward the trash pile. At the same instant the burglar broke from cover, blasting through the discarded boxes. The chase was on again, but this time Tony was ready.

In two steps he was behind the fleeing figure–and gaining. He reached out and grabbed the thief's coat, locking his fingers tightly around the collar. Then he dropped into a pile of trash, pulling the straining runner down with him.

"Help! Police!" called the struggling captive.

"Yeah, call for help," Tony shot back. "Then explain why you're carrying around a computer keyboard with no computer or—"

The word caught in Tony's throat. For the first time he could see clearly the smooth skin and soft curve of his captive's face. Strands of long curly brown hair had popped out from under the old knit cap covering the person's head.

"Hey," the boy gasped, "you're a *girl!*"

Tony saw dark eyes stare up at him coldly. "So? What is *that* supposed to mean?"

Tony shifted uneasily. "Well, I don't want to hurt you or anything. It's just that you've got my keyboard and—"

"Here, take it!" the girl said harshly, handing it over to Tony and getting to her feet. Then she added, "And for your information, I've been chased by bigger and meaner people than you. My father, for one, before Mother and I ran away from him."

"Really?" Tony asked, a strange feeling coming over him as he realized that he was holding an almost polite conversation with someone who had just tried to commit a crime against him. He also noticed an unfamiliar accent accompanying the girl's voice.

The thief waved her hand. "Look, just take your stupid key-whatever and leave me alone, OK? I probably couldn't pawn it anyway if it's supposed to come with a computer."

Tony turned his attention to the keyboard, giving it a quick once-over. He looked back at the girl and spoke again. "You really don't know much about computers, do you? I guess I thought everyone did."

The girl sneered. "I haven't had much chance to learn

about computers. I spend most of my time looking for food—and running away from people like you."

Tony grinned, ignoring her last statement. "You should be nice to me. Not only do I know about computers, but I also know there's a police officer walking a beat not far from here."

The girl paused. "I need to go—my mother worries."

"Wait," said Tony suddenly. "Tell me your name."

The girl sighed wearily. "Olena," she said. "It's Russian."

"My name's Tony," the boy announced. "Where do you live?"

Olena looked at her companion. She saw goodness in his face, and her dark eyes filled with a strange sadness. She hung her head slightly. "Everywhere," she said. "And nowhere."

"Whattaya mean?" Tony asked.

The girl didn't answer. She just turned and walked away.

Tony, sensing that getting the police involved would accomplish little, watched as she walked quickly from the alley.

---

* *Voyager* was Tony's time-travel machine in which he visited Bible times to learn more about Jesus.

CHAPTER 02

HOMELESS AND HOPELESS

Mr. Lester looked up from his work as Tony entered the room pulling a cart burdened with computer equipment. The boy jumped when he saw the man.

"Oh, you scared me," he gasped.

"Why?" asked Mr. Lester, adjusting his thick glasses and squinting toward the door. "It should come as no shock to you that I'm in my workshop, where I belong, doing what I'm being paid very little to do."

Tony smiled. "You're absolutely right," he said, guiding the cart between rows of work tables piled high with circuit boards, empty computer cases, burned-out power supplies, and malfunctioning hard drives. "I figured you'd be gone. It's after quitting time."

The middle-aged African-American man squinted at the clock hanging slightly askew on the wall. "So it is," he said, beginning to put his tools away and straighten the collection of chips and cables littering his desk. "Did my backup server work for you?" asked Mr. Lester, eyeing Tony's cartload. "And the projectors and those reportedly faulty external hard drives?"

Tony nodded. "You're a good man, Mr. Lester. Thanks!"

He watched as the technician rubbed the bridge of his nose, forcing his glasses to wobble against his forehead. "By the way," the man added, "while you're putting away the equipment from your cart, you might want to check out the box by the window. It's memory chips from Korea. They're in groupings of 128 megs. Got a great deal on 'em."

Tony closed his eyes and savored the announcement. "One hundred twenty-eight megs . . ." He spoke the words as if each was of great value. "That oughta move a few cows."

Mr. Lester blinked. He opened his mouth to speak, then closed it. "I don't want to know," he mumbled.

Tony laughed. "It's just an experiment."

"Do I want to hear this?" asked Mr. Lester, half joking. "I hope I'm doing the right thing by letting you use company equipment in exchange for a little help after school. I'm not interested in your crazy VR research. Besides, what you do when you're not in this room is your business, not mine."

Tony leaned toward the man. "I made haze," he said.

"You did?" Mr. Lester gasped.

"Yup. Zones 3 and 4. You could almost smell it. Covered an entire hillside with the stuff, just like when sunlight slants through atmospheric moisture. It was incredible."

"Someday men in starched uniforms are gonna come and whisk you away and I'll have to explain to your parents that I lent you the equipment to run your idiotic tests."

"And birds," Tony whispered.

"Birds?" Mr. Lester breathed. "You made birds fly in 3-D?"

"Fly and sing!"

"That's it. Your scaring me! I'm outta here." The man hurriedly gathered up his satchel. "I've written your job assignment for this afternoon. Eighteenth floor is having network problems. Probably in the router. Forget about cows and singing birds and concentrate on your job, OK?" He turned to leave, then paused. "What kind of birds?"

"Hawks," Tony whispered. "Fast ones."

"I'm not hearing this!" the man shouted over his shoulder as he ran from the room, slamming the door behind him.

Tony chuckled as he finished unloading the cart. Checking the clock, he decided he had an hour and a half to work before hunger and the thought of steaming hot vegetarian meatballs would drive him from the building to the apartment complex two blocks away.

He flipped the switch of the computer resting on the repair stand and waited for it to boot up.

As the main network-testing application loaded itself into memory, Tony noticed the symbol of a mailbox flashing on and off at the bottom right-hand corner of the screen, indicating that he had unread e-mail waiting.

Tony grinned. Perhaps it was a note from Grandma Parks, who lived in Winnetka, a peaceful suburb north of Chicago. The message was probably filled with its usual ramblings of all the exciting events that had taken place at the retirement village during the last couple of days. Tony enjoyed every word, not because he was into crafts, indoor flower gardening, or the latest village gossip. He simply loved his grandmother. That's why he'd installed an old computer in her room and patiently taught her how to operate it.

Grandma Parks wrote several times each week, revealing in great detail and with copious amounts of humor all that went on in her peaceful corner of the world. To Tony, it was better than TV.

Grabbing the computer mouse, the boy clicked on the symbol. In a few seconds, lines of words appeared on the screen, words the boy knew immediately hadn't been written by his grandmother.

"Did you catch her?" the message asked. Then it stated flatly, "You can't trust a Russian."

Tony stared at the message, a frown creasing his young brow. Did the writer know about his recent encounter with the girl in the alley?

Glancing down at the signature line, he noticed a handwritten graphic scrawled across the screen. In glowing red letters, it read "Dark Angel."

Olena paused at the front door of the shelter, eyeing the collection of occupants carefully. There'd be a sizable crowd tonight because the weather forecaster had predicted six inches of fresh snow.

An old woman approached, her face twisted into a scowl. "She took my brush. She took my brush!" she shouted.

"Who?" Olena asked.

"Your mother. She took it, and now she's gone."

"Gone where?"

The old woman thrust gnarled and stained hands out in front of her. "What do I look like, a travel agent? You just stay outta my way and keep your hands off my stuff."

Olena ran to the back of the shelter and stopped at the spot where she and her mother had spent the past few nights. The space beside her blanket was empty, save for a small scrap of paper stuck between two floorboards. The girl reached down and lifted the note. In the fading light she struggled to make out the rough, handwritten words. "Olena. I go now to far away. Don't be sad. Maybe I come back if I earn money. Please believe me that I love you, and someday you forgive me too. Mama."

The last hint of daylight touched the girl's face as a tear slipped down her cheek. She gazed out the window at the softening silhouettes of the buildings and listened to the roar of passing traffic. Now she was truly alone. Now she'd have to face the future with no hand to hold and no voice to encourage.

Olena sank to the floor, hungry, confused, terrified.

"You keep away from my things," the old woman called from across the room. "Your mother was a thief, and you're a thief. That's all you'll ever be."

The girl wept, lost in a world without hope.

Tony and Tie Li sat with their legs dangling from the cement wall separating Chicago from Lake Michigan. Behind them, traffic on Lake Shore Drive flowed steadily, adding a distant rumble to the sound of water brushing against the barrier.

Grant Park boasted few visitors this cold January day,

leaving its snowy pathways and icy benches to the bundled joggers who hurried by and the occasional shivering tourist gesturing in wonder at the towering buildings rising to the west.

This was the siblings' favorite spot, a place where they could turn their backs on the city and gaze at the endless horizon stretching across the brow of the frigid lake. Sometimes a whistling wind and rush of waves would drown out the drone of traffic, allowing the youngsters' imaginations to hear the cry of crows or the distant mooing of cattle. But on this day Chicago's presence was quite recognizable, even under layers of earmuffs and scarves.

"I wonder what happened," Tie Li said.

"When?" Tony asked.

"In Jerusalem."

The boy frowned. "What are you talking about?"

Tie Li glanced at her brother. "Remember? After the tomb was empty?"

Tony nodded slowly. It had been their last journey in *Voyager,* before the tornado had uprooted their lives forever.

"He said He'd come back," the boy responded.

"Yeah." Tie Li sighed. "I guess we'll never know."

The two sat in silence for a long moment. "Did people just sort of forget about the Man who talked about peace and healed the sick?" the girl wondered aloud.

Tony shrugged. "There are still churches around. People sing and pray and stuff. You know, like Grandma."

"But," Tie Li said, "it's not like He said it would be. He promised He'd make the world like the garden again, remember? He told people that if they'd believe in what He taught, they'd have a beautiful new home. Why hasn't that happened?"

Tony shook his head, reliving their incredible adventures together as they searched the past for answers to life's most troubling questions. They'd discovered why the world had become so filled with hate and violence. They'd seen the terrible damage sin had caused generations and nations. And while their journeys in *Voyager* had provided many answers, they'd raised questions as well. What had happened to the people who chose to believe in the man called Jesus? What about His promises of a beautiful world to come, where suffering and pain would be forgotten, where peace would rule the entire universe?

The boy frowned. The Book he'd used to guide their adventures had told of people in Jerusalem who'd been touched by what seemed to be little flames of fire. After that, they'd talked in other languages, healed the sick, and helped hundreds of people believe in Jesus. What had happened to them, and the power behind the mysterious flames that had sparked their lives so long ago?

"Do you know what I wish?" Tie Li sighed, interrupting her brother's thoughts.

"What?"

The girl turned. "I wish we could see what happened after Jesus left."

Tony ground his heel against the wall. *"Voyager's* gone," he said quietly.

Tie Li nodded. "But *you* aren't."

The boy studied his sister's face. In her eyes he saw a

familiar confidence, an unshakable belief that he could do anything on earth. Anything.

"Tie Li," he said, "I . . . can't build another machine like *Voyager*. I just can't."

His sister looked out across the frozen expanse of Lake Michigan. "Don't you want to know what happened?" she asked.

"Yes, of course I do. I want to know why Jesus hasn't come back. I want to know why we're still here, and why Grandma's getting older and older while she keeps saying that Jesus might come tomorrow or next week or next year. She's been telling me that ever since I was a little kid."

The girl shrugged. "Then let's *look* for the answers. You and me. If you can put facts and stuff into your computers and make it seem like we're back at the farm, can't you do that for any place, and—"

"And . . . any *time*." Tony spoke the words in a whisper, not believing his own announcement. From the Book and history, he certainly gathered enough data. Could the technology known as virtual reality help them learn more about God's hand in history?

Watching the snow blow across the icy face of the lake, the boy lowered his gaze. Tie Li grinned. She'd seen that look before, that calculating stare showing that her brother was totally immersed in some complicated and unexplainable line of thought. She sat quietly, listening to the muffled sound of traffic drifting in the distance. The last time she'd seen Tony's face etched with such an expression, the end result had been a machine capable of carrying them to scenes long lost to history. She could only imagine what would spring from her sibling's latest mind-journey into the high-tech world of computers.

The very next afternoon Tony burst into the workroom and tossed his backpack on a table. Mr. Lester glanced up from the circuit board he was studying under a lighted magnifier positioned near his chin.

"Hi, Tony," he called.

"Got a question for you," the young boy said as he grabbed a chair and moved close to his companion.

"I'm fine; how are you?" the man with the thick glasses responded with a smile.

Tony grinned shyly. "Oh, I'm sorry. Hello, Mr. Lester. You're looking wonderful, Mr. Lester. How are the kids, Mr. Lester? How's Mrs. Lester, Mr. Lester?"

The technician shook his head. "There are no kids, there is no Mrs. Lester, and I think I'm getting scarlet fever."

Tony blinked. "You're getting what?

"I need a good disease," the man sighed. "Administration won't give me any sick days for normal afflictions such as colds and flu. They want me gasping for breath and begging for pain relievers before they'll let me outta here."

Tony shook his head as if to clear his thoughts. "Mr. Lester, I gotta ask you some important questions."

"OK," the man sighed. "Since I may, or may not, have scarlet fever, ask."

Tony looked one way, then another. His companion did the same, then frowned.

"You know I've been experimenting with virtual reality, right?" the boy said.

"Yes."

"Well, I need a lot more processing power and tons of memory."

"How much?"

"All of it."

"*All* of it?"

"I want to tap the entire network of this company—you know, make it my core processor by connecting everything together as if it were one big computer."

"Can't be done," the man stated flatly. "These systems are busy all day. Computers keep this company running."

"But," Tony said, moving even closer, "in the evenings everyone goes home. The equipment is idle, right?"

"More or less . . . "

"So if I can tie all the processing power in the building together and connect it to the Internet, I should be able to have the most powerful electronic brain in the city. I could gather information from anywhere in the world, from any database, from any archive, and project the results using my 3-D translators."

Mr. Lester shook his head. "Something as powerful as what you're planning would be a threat to national security, to say nothing of my pension."

"I need a room," Tony continued. "A big room in this building, so I can run direct transfer lines to my projectors."

Mr. Lester glanced at the boy. "You mean like the thirty-sixth floor? They haven't even finished it yet. The outside walls and insulation are up, but there are no interior studs." The man paused, then added, "Of course, there is power up there. And that space isn't scheduled for occupancy for another year."

"The whole floor?" asked Tony, wide-eyed.

"You'd have to program the elevator to go that high. Right now it stops at 35." He looked at Tony. "I could probably get permission to use the area."

Tony gasped. "Perfect!"

Mr. Lester tilted his head. "What is it, exactly, that you want to accomplish?" he asked.

Tony hesitated. What he was about to say was utterly bizarre, even by his own standards.

CHAPTER 03

GETTING READY

Tony studied Mr. Lester's face, trying to decide just how to respond to the man's question.

"I . . . uh . . . I want to find a missing person," he said.

"Yeah? Who?"

"A Man."

"How long's he been missing?"

The boy wrinkled his nose. "About . . . 2,000 years?"

"Two thou—" Mr. Lester gasped. "Tony Parks, you're crazy. Computers are the next best thing to antacids, but they can't raise the dead."

"They don't have to," the boy said with a grin. "This missing Person has already been resurrected. I saw the empty tomb."

"Oh, boy, here we go!" Mr. Lester declared, throwing up his hands. "I'm not listening anymore. Nope. I don't hear you. You're totally bonkers, my friend, and at such a young age, too."

"No, I'm not," Tony countered, "just curious. Aren't you interested in what I'm doing?"

"No way! You're on your own. Just do your thing and

keep poor ol' overworked and underpaid Mr. Lester out of it."

"All right," the boy sighed. "But, it's going to be *sooo* cool."

The man returned to his repair project. "What? Did you say something? I'm sorry; I only talk to *sane* people."

Tony chuckled and headed for his workbench. Things were definitely looking up. He had the space, the computer hardware, and the time. Now all he needed was a master program to pull everything together.

His eyes fell on his device resting on the table. *Wait a minute,* he thought to himself. *How 'bout SIMON? It's a rather simple information-gathering computer right now. Not much artificial intelligence programmed in. But perhaps there could be more.*

"Excuse me for a minute," Tony called over his shoulder as he hurried toward the door, the device held tightly in his hand. "I need to check on something. Be right back."

Mr. Lester looked about the room. "There's that voice again. I wonder where it's coming from."

Tony was still grinning when he stepped into the storage room at the end of the hallway. Placing the device on a shelf in front of him, he flipped two switches and pressed a button. The last thing he wanted to do was let Mr. Lester see him talking to a computer. It would drive the poor man insane.

"SIMON?" the boy said.

"SIMON standing by," came the droning response.

Tony thought for a minute and then said clearly, "State your programmed search range."

He heard the device click a couple of times. "Search range limited to office network and local phone lines."

The boy nodded. "Continue."

Unseen mechanisms whirled again. "To generate searches beyond present boundaries . . . SIMON requires direct access to the Internet . . . through dedicated T1 lines as well as storage capabilities not yet assigned."

Tony drew in a deep breath. "OK. SIMON, calculate suggested code for creating an internal data-gathering program to expand SIMON capabilities for *global* access."

A light on the device flickered on and off as the software created a response to the boy's command.

"SIMON has calculated the needed code. Ready to download."

"Great," the boy said softly. Then speaking to the computer again, he commanded, "Hold all information in your RAM banks." *I'll connect SIMON to a printer later,* Tony thought.

"Data on hold," the device stated.

Tony's mind whirled with breathtaking contemplations. Would it really be possible to do what he wanted to do? Since leaving the farm, he'd had very little to motivate him. At the farm all that he cared about in the whole world outside of his family had been housed in his little workshop at the base of the barn. Now, if his creative thoughts would flow as before, he and Tie Li could examine history through virtual reality by using real-time as well as stored data gathered from around the world. The challenge thrilled him.

Tony grinned broadly as he picked up his device and

headed back toward the computer room. For the first time in a long time he felt like the day was worth living.

Days melted into each other like wax at the base of a burning candle. Tony spent every available minute seated before his precious computer, entering long lines of code into SIMON's memory, testing, retesting, making adjustments, until it responded with blinding speed and total accuracy to his every command. He programmed new words and phrases into SIMON's artificial intelligence, expanding its ability to understand his commands.

Finally the big day arrived. All was ready. Tony was about to put his new program and carefully constructed equipment to the ultimate test.

"Tie Li, will you come with me to my work area?" the boy asked his sister late one afternoon. "I want to show you something really, really awesome. You're gonna love it."

The girl smiled as she and Tony made their way toward the towering office building two blocks away. "I know I'm going to like this," she said, doing her best to keep up. "You made it, didn't you?"

Tony grinned. His adopted sister always thought he was wonderful. It felt good to be trusted and admired like that.

The lobby at the base of the building was emptying fast. Feet scurried across the bright tiled floor as workers who'd completed their day's labors headed home.

Stepping into the elevator, Tony looked around to

make sure no one was watching. He pressed the button for level 35, then pushed the "door close" and "door open" buttons simultaneously. The light illuminating the thirty-fifth-floor selector blinked off, and a flashing light indicated that level 36 had been activated.

Tie Li frowned. "How did that happen?"

Tony leaned forward and whispered, "Magic."

As the cubicle began to elevate, Tony couldn't help smiling. SIMON had performed perfectly during the past few days, sniffing through mammoth data bases, scouring art and photography archives around the world, scanning millions of written words in dozens of languages, examining ancient writings and archaeology findings stored on university and government networks, leaving no electronic stone unturned in its quest to gather all known information on the subjects Tony had listed.

The boy had added one final touch just the night before. With growing excitement he'd placed a shiny CD into a computer connected directly to SIMON's input port, downloading in a matter of seconds the complete text of the Bible in seven versions and four languages, including the original Greek and Hebrew.

It was now up to SIMON and the astonishing processing power of an entire corporate network to arrange the data and translate it into clear, recognizable images before feeding them through a series of projectors that formed the multimedia backbone of Tony's virtual reality experiment.

The very thought of what was about to happen caused the boy's feet to dance as he waited for the elevator to reach the unused and totally ignored thirty-sixth floor of the tall Chicago office building.

The elevator jolted to a stop, and the door slid open. Sweeping his hand out in front of him, Tony announced, "Tie Li, welcome to VR-2002, a place like no other in the entire world!"

The girl chuckled as she walked around small piles of discarded building supplies. "Looks like empty office space to me. Sure could use some decorating—and a few walls."

Tony grinned. "Let's just say we're about to 'decorate' this place like it's never been decorated before."

His companion studied a bank of projectors positioned along a far wall. "What will we see, Tony?" she asked. "What are we looking for?"

The boy walked up beside his sister. "Answers," he said softly. "Answers to the questions you asked that day by the lake. I want to know if anyone continued to believe what Jesus said after He went back to heaven. I want to know what we should be thinking now, today, right here in Chicago. Is He *really* coming back? Did He mean everything He said? I've gotta know." He hesitated. "Sometimes, well, I don't have a lot of hope. I get kinda discouraged—know what I mean?"

"Yeah," Tie Li agreed. "I know."

"So," the boy responded, his excitement returning, "are you ready to dig around in the past? Or at least the past that SIMON has put together for us?"

"I'm ready!" Tie Li nodded enthusiastically.

The boy held the device out in front of him. "SIMON," he called, "begin simulation A39, full effects. Use all available processing power."

"Simulation under way," the device responded instantly.

In the blink of an eye, what had been a high, cobweb-encrusted ceiling became a dark sky filled with boiling storm clouds. Lightning flashed and thunder boomed. His virtual recreation was underway!

So sudden was the transformation that Tie Li screamed, but a shrieking, gale-force gust of wind sucked the sound from her throat. In the distance, amid what looked like angry, crashing waves, a wooden ship swayed drunkenly in the shallows by the shore, smashing against jagged rocks, its bow boards separating as towering masts snapped like matchsticks.

In horror she saw pieces of wreckage tumbling onto a beach. There seemed to be people clinging to the boards. Tie Li turned, then gasped. Her brother was gone.

"Tony!" she called out. The roar of the wind was nearly deafening, and lightning punctuated the sky, accompanied by a steady, earthshaking bellow of thunder. Tie Li's senses were assaulted with the almost overpowering forces around her.

"Tony!"

"Over here," came a distant reply.

She could just make out her brother standing by the shoreline, where virtual waves swept across the sands.

As the girl hurried in his direction, she spotted the form of a man stumbling up from the breakers. His hair and beard were soaked, his clothes clinging to his frail body in torn shreds. "Don't worry!" he shouted to a group of men huddled farther up the beach.

Another man joined him, gasping for breath. "Are you OK?" he shouted above the gale.

"Yes. Everyone made it. I told you they would."

The second man shook his head. "How, Paul? How did you know?"

"The God that I serve is wise and can see into the future," came the quick reply. "If He tells me something, I believe it, and He told me that everyone would make it safely to shore."

The second survivor glanced out at the sinking ship, then at the speaker. "You're still my prisoner, you know," he said.

"I know, Julius," came the gentle reply. "God has work for me to do in Rome. He's using you to take me there."

"You should've tried to escape," Julius insisted. "Once you arrive in Rome, I doubt you'll leave alive."

The man in the tattered and torn clothes gazed at the angry sea. "I'm part of a movement not even the emperor can silence. You can beat me, burn my flesh, throw me in jail, and even take my life, but the words of my Lord will continue to spread far beyond Rome." He turned to his companion. "But for now, let's get everyone gathered up and find shelter. I don't know about you, but I could use a good meal spread on a table that's not tilting back and forth. How about it, Julius? Even prisoners must eat."

The gentleman at his side nodded. "All right, Paul. Let's get busy." The two men walked away, stumbling around broken pieces of wreckage. "First of all, we must find out where on earth we are. Oh, and don't be too trusting of the soldiers in my command. They wanted to kill you on the boat."

"I know," Paul admitted. "Thank you for defending me. Most Roman centurions would not have done so."

Tie Li watched the men walk along the shoreline, reviving prone figures still clinging to broken pieces of the ship. Tony joined his sister.

"Who are they?" she asked, leaning close to her brother so he could hear her question.

"That's Paul the apostle," he said. "He's being taken to Rome to stand trial."

"Trial for what?"

Tony glanced at his sister. "For preaching about Jesus, for saying that God's way is the best way to live. My research showed that he wrote a lot of letters trying to convince his readers to keep believing in God and not give up hope for a new world to come. The shipwreck took place about 2,000 years ago on the island of Malta, in the Mediterranean Sea."

Tie Li shielded her eyes from the driving rain. "What happened to him?"

Tony studied the distant form that lovingly helped struggling survivors to higher ground. "He had his day in court," he said. "Lots of them, actually. Finally he appeared before a man named Nero."

"And?"

Tony looked at his sister. "And he ordered Paul's death."

Tie Li gasped. "Why?"

"Because he refused to stop talking about Jesus."

"Hey!" said Tie Li suddenly, looking at her brother. "I

thought we were going to look for answers together. You seem to know a lot about this already!"

Tony laughed. "Well, I learned a lot when entering data into SIMON's so-called brain. But just because I know a lot of *facts* doesn't mean I know a lot of *answers*. We're still in this search together."

Tie Li nodded.

Tony lifted the electronic device from his belt. "SIMON," he called, holding the box close to his mouth, "end simulation."

In a flash the two were standing in a quiet empty space. "Lights," the boy ordered.

As rows of bulbs flickered on, Tie Li shook her head slowly. After a long pause, she spoke. "That was incredible . . ."

Her brother smiled with satisfaction.

"Tony," Tie Li continued, "that man on the beach. He really believed in what he was saying. You could see it in his eyes."

Tony nodded, then turned and walked to the far wall where he tapped several commands into a keyboard. "One thing's for sure," he called, "Paul certainly hadn't forgotten what Jesus taught. He was willing to be shipwrecked, imprisoned, and killed for his beliefs."

The boy stiffened as he read a message on his computer screen.

"What is it?" Tie Li asked, walking in his direction.

Tony jammed SIMON into his backpack and hurried toward the elevator door. "Come on," he called, ignoring her question, "I . . . I need to do something. Go home and tell Mom and Dad I'll be there in about an hour, OK?"

As the elevator door closed, the lights in the room clicked off, leaving the large empty space bathed in shadows, the darkness punctuated only by the soft brilliance of the computer screen. In glowing letters was a message in a small, bordered box. "The Russian girl has been arrested," it said. "What are you going to do about it?" It was signed *Dark Angel.*

CHAPTER 04

CAUGHT
BY THE POLICE

now was falling heavily as Tony stared out the window of the taxi. Most of the city was bathed in its own artificial light, but there still remained a glow to the west, where the sun was setting beyond the clouds.

The computer-wise teenager was occasionally called away to work on some mysterious malady in the company's computer network, so he knew his parents wouldn't worry about him for at least a couple of hours. He had asked Tie Li to tell them that he'd be back soon after he finished looking into a matter across town. By then he hoped to have the situation in hand.

He lifted a device to his lips and spoke quietly so as not to draw the attention of the driver. "SIMON," he whispered, "cellular connect. Update report concerning Russian girl."

Tony listened intently as a familiar electronic voice responded. "Police reports indicate subject at West Harrison Street precinct."

The boy drummed his fingers on his knee, remembering the curt message that had appeared on his computer screen back on the thirty-sixth floor of his father's office building: "The Russian girl has been detained by police. What are you going to do about it?" It had been signed by "Dark Angel," the same mysterious writer who'd posted a message several weeks back. Apparently, this person had access to the city's police data network, something only an experienced computer hacker could accomplish.

"SIMON," the boy whispered, the device held close to his face. "Trace the Dark Angel message."

After a moment he heard, "Unable. Router switches re-programmed. SIMON standing by."

Tony's eyes narrowed. The hacker was good, even able to cover his electronic tracks after sending a message. But how did he know about the girl he'd met in the alley two weeks before?

The taxi pulled up in front of police headquarters just as an officer was leading a young woman to a waiting squad car. Tony jumped out even before the cab had come to a stop, and raced toward the pair.

"Olena!" he called, almost slipping on a stretch of ice. "Where have you been?"

The girl looked up in surprise, and the officer's hand paused halfway to the door handle.

Tony skidded to a halt and smiled broadly at the po-liceman. "I'll take her back with me. You don't have to bother driving her, uh, home."

The man frowned. "You know this girl?"

"Yeah. Well, kinda. I mean, she's a friend, sorta."

The girl's eyebrows rose slightly. "Yes, officer. This is my friend . . . "

"My name is Tony Parks," the boy interrupted, speaking to the officer. "If you were going to take Olena home, I'd be happy to pay her fare, and she can ride with me."

Just then an emergency message crackled out over the police car's radio. A look of concern crossed the officer's face as he listened intently to it. Walking briskly to the driver's side of the car, he called over the roof to Olena.

"Young lady, I have an emergency call. I'm only going to give you a warning this time. Don't let us find you trying to stow away on any more interstate buses, understand?"

"Yes, sir," the girl said, a restrained smile of relief playing about her mouth.

The two young people watched as the police car's rooftop lights lit up and the officer sped away.

Inside the cab, Olena turned to her companion. "You're the boy from the alley, right?"

"Yes."

"How did you know where I was and what was going on?"

"I'll tell you later," Tony said. "But first I promised to take you home."

Olena frowned. "I don't have a home," she said quietly.

"I know," said Tony. "You told me. You live nowhere."

"I really mean it," the girl said, hurt and shame reflected on her face. "I don't have anyplace to go."

Tony looked across the rear seat at the girl. "Not true," he said with a smile.

Snow swirled about the car as it drove through the streets, heading back into the heart of the city.

Mrs. Parks looked up from her cooking just as Tony entered the kitchen. The rich aroma of steaming vegetables filled the room. "Hey, Ma," her son called with a smile.

Immediately behind him came a young girl with curly brown hair and dark, sober eyes. "Hello," she said cautiously.

The woman stopped stirring. "Well, hello," she responded, her face registering surprise.

"So," Tony said, sniffing at the vapor rising above the pot, "we're having stir fry for supper? Great! We're hungry—right, Olena?"

The girl nodded shyly.

The two left the kitchen, leaving Mrs. Parks standing, eyebrows raised, by the stove.

In the living room Mr. Parks sat reading the evening newspaper, enjoying the warmth of the gas fire flickering in the fake-stone hearth. He was turning a page when he saw his son and a girl walk in nervously from the kitchen.

Tie Li, who was giggling at something she was reading, glanced up and paused in midchuckle.

"Hello, everyone," Tony called with a wave. "It's nice and warm in the apartment tonight. That's good."

"Uh, Tony?" said Mrs. Parks, following the pair into the living room.

"Yes, Ma?"

The woman cleared her throat. "Will we be having company for supper?"

Tony smiled. "If it's OK."

"Could you introduce us to your friend? I don't believe we've met her before."

The boy nodded. "Mom, Dad, Tie Li, this is Olena. She, uh, doesn't have a home."

Mrs. Parks blinked.

"So, um, I was wondering if she could stay here for a little while—until her mom gets back." Mr. and Mrs. Parks stared at each other, surprised. Olena hung her head in embarrassment.

"Where did your mother go?" Tony's father inquired.

"I'm not sure," answered Olena. "Maybe Texas or Arkansas."

Tie Li stood and walked over to the girl. "Where's your dad?"

"We haven't seen him for more than a year," said Olena nervously. Then she blurted out, "I don't want to be a bother. I can go back to the shelter."

"No!" Tony interrupted. His face reddened as he glanced about the room. "I mean, no. That's not a safe place. Remember that woman who was mad at you? You said she could go crazy and hurt you or something."

"What woman?" asked Dad, putting down his paper.

"There's room in my bedroom," Tie Li offered enthusiastically. "And she could ride on the el* with Tony and me when we go to school."

Mr. Parks spoke again. "Let's all sit down. I think we need to get more information here and have one of our 'family councils.'"

"What is your name again?" Mrs. Parks asked.

"Olena," the girl said softly.

"That's Russian," Tony added, "just like her."

"I'm from Vietnam," Tie Li interjected. "And Tony's

great-grandfather was from Romania, and Mrs. Parks's mother is from Sweden. Looks like we've got the whole world living in this apartment!"

After a lengthy discussion and a lot of probing questions, Mr. Parks said, "Well, Mother, what do you think?"

"I agree to let Olena stay with us for a couple of days after we phone the city's Social Services Department, just in case someone needs to find her."

"No, wait!" Tony said, lifting his hand.

Mr. Parks frowned. "Why, Tony? Is there something more about Olena we need to know?"

Tony nervously licked his lips. "No, Dad. There's nothing secret about Olena. It's just that, well, she needs to be here instead of out there." He pointed in the direction of the window and the city lights beyond. "Besides, I . . . already listed her with Social Services."

"You *what?*" exclaimed his mother. "Isn't this something you should have talked to us about first?"

"I apologize that I didn't phone you first. I guess you raised me to look out for other people. And things were happening so fast," Tony offered sincerely.

"I guess it's OK this time, Tony," said Mr. Parks. "But promise us that in the future you'll always check with us before acting so hastily about something this important."

"I promise."

"Well," Mrs. Parks sighed, "all we can do is go on from here. Tell us about your contact with Social Services."

"I registered her under our address and also gave your office information, Dad."

"I'm sure they'll call to verify," the man said. He thought for a minute. "Well, I guess everything seems to be in order. Olena is basically visiting us for a while, so there are no legal issues to work out. And you've made it possible for her mother to find her when she returns."

Olena smiled broadly. "Thank you," she said. "I won't be a bother. I promise."

"Come," Tie Li offered happily. "I'll show you my . . . I mean *our* room."

As the two girls left, Mr. Parks glanced over at his son. "First it was squirrels and baby birds. Now it's people?"

The boy grinned sheepishly. "Take after my mom and dad, huh?"

"Are you sure about her, son?" asked Mrs. Parks.

"She has *no one,*" Tony stated. "Her mom abandoned her a couple of weeks ago—just left her in the city like an old shoe she didn't want anymore. She might not ever come back! But I couldn't let Olena just roam the streets forever."

Mrs. Parks sat down beside her son. "Tony, you have a wonderful, caring heart. But homeless people can be trouble."

"Where did you meet her?" his father wanted to know.

Tony cleared his throat. "We kinda ran into each other in an alley."

"In an alley?"

"Don't worry, Dad. I was just chasing her." Tony's cheeks flushed. His story was sounding worse every second!

"*Chasing* her? But why?"

"She stole my keyboard and, well, I was trying to get it back."

Mr. and Mrs. Parks stared at each other for a moment, then shook their heads.

"I love my caring son," Mrs. Parks said, "but I don't always understand him."

Mr. Parks added in a serious tone, "I hope we're doing the right thing."

Olena lay between the soft sheets of her bed, marveling at the delicious silence of the room. The evening meal had been the best she'd tasted in a long, long time.

But it wasn't just the food and warmth that made her feel so wonderful. It was something else, something she couldn't identify.

Slipping from beneath the covers, she walked to the window and stared out at the city streets far below. Even in her joy, there was an ache in her heart that fireplaces, steaming plates of stir-fry vegetables, and friendly faces couldn't satisfy. In spite of everything that had happened, she still felt lonely and wondered why.

Her gaze followed the shoreline as it swept past the dark outlines of Meigs Field and Rainbow Beach. In the far distance the lights of Gary, Indiana, illuminated the high clouds.

Somewhere, out beyond the horizon, was her mother, probably shivering in a shelter or lying abandoned in some dirty motel room, alone and penniless. Yes. That was keeping her from fully enjoying the loving, gentle people she'd met earlier in the evening.

A hand touched her shoulder. She turned to see Tie Li standing in the shadows behind her. "You're missing your mom, aren't you," the girl stated.

"Yes."

Her companion sighed. "I lost my mom and dad in a war. Then I found Tony, and he made me happy again. Hey, if you want him to, he might be able to find your mom. Tony's pretty smart. He can do amazing things with his computers."

Olena shook her head. "I don't know if my mother *wants* to be found. She's running away, you know."

"From what?"

The girl's breath caught in her throat as she fought back tears. "From me," she said.

The next afternoon Tony arrived at work, whistling. Mr. Lester looked up from the innards of a computer case and scowled. "What's that awful noise?"

The boy paused, then grinned. "Me. I was whistling."

"Is that what that was?" the man asked. "I thought someone was letting the air out of a tire."

Tony shrugged. "Sorry. I thought I was staying on tune pretty good. If you'd rather, I could sing."

"No. I've heard you do that, too. Whistling's better."

The boy settled himself at his workbench and studied the assignment sheet thoughtfully. "Again?" he gasped, noticing a nearby machine with a strange dark stain on its front panel.

"There are those in accounting who think internal CD-ROM players make great coffee cup holders," Mr. Lester sighed. "Let's hope they're better with numbers than they are with computer equipment. Seems one of their secretaries tried to load four ounces of decaf into her hard drive. I gave them a replacement machine, and you can have the honor of cleaning that one out for her. I asked if she wanted cream with her spreadsheet. She was not amused."

Tony laughed. "Of course we can't forget about the guy who wanted to remind himself to take a floppy disk to the office with him so he fastened it to his refrigerator with a magnet. Completely wiped out the data."

Mr. Lester shook his head. "Earthlings. They're all such earthlings."

With that, the two focused their attention on the afternoon tasks, laying skillful hands on malfunctioning pieces of equipment, working their electronic magic on the circuit boards and processing units so important to the company.

Just before quitting time Mr. Lester glanced up from his work. "Hey, Tony?"

"Yeah?"

"How's your little experiment coming along? You know, the one I don't want to know anything about?"

"Fine," the boy stated.

"I noticed you haven't disrupted any part of the network in the building. I appreciate that."

"I'm being careful."

"Good."

All at once, a little mailbox appeared at the bottom right-hand corner of Tony's screen. The boy grabbed his mouse and clicked on the symbol. A message appeared.

"Olena's mother is in jail. I'll contact you later this evening with more information." As before, it was signed "Dark Angel."

Tony glanced at Mr. Lester busily concentrating on a set of wires running from the back of a network server. Tony felt a bit frightened. Whoever this Dark Angel was, he or she seemed to be very interested in Olena and anyone close to her. He also seemed to be very cunning at gathering sensitive data from distant networks. To track down a person took experience and a deep understanding of how databases are constructed. This type of person could be helpful or dangerous, depending on which side of the law they happened to be.

"Something wrong?"

Tony turned to see Mr. Lester staring at him.

"Uh, not really," the boy said. "Just finishing up. If it's OK with you, I'd like to leave a few minutes early tonight."

Mr. Lester nodded his approval and Tony hurried from the room.

---

*El is an abbreviation for the elevated public transit system in Chicago, Illinois.

CHAPTER 05

SWAMP MONSTERS

Tony knocked gently on Tie Li's bedroom door. His face showed deep concern for the girl he knew waited inside the room, a person he cared for in spite of his misgivings about her past and uncertain future.

"Enter at your own risk," came a giggly reply.

Tony frowned. What did that mean?

Opening the door he peeked inside then jumped back in fright. Two young women who resembled Tie Li and Olena sat on the end of one of the beds, staring back at him, their faces covered with a green pasty substance, their hair wrapped tightly around large curlers, and their hands dripping with what looked and smelled like honey.

"We want to be beautiful," Tie Li called, her words somewhat muffled by a strange contraption filling her mouth. "Even our teeth will be whiter because of this stuff I ordered from TV."

Tony wrinkled his nose and tried hard not to laugh. "You look like swamp monsters," he said.

Olena grinned around her own mouth-filling gadget. "Would you like to try the mud bath or soothing honey lotion?"

"I don't wanna put gunk on any part of my body," Tony chuckled.

Tie Li turned stiffly to her friend. "How long are we supposed to leave this goop on?"

"I don't know," Olena shrugged. "How long has it been?"

"I don't know," Tie Li mumbled. "Maybe we should wash it off now."

The two struggled to their feet and waddled toward the bathroom. Tony shook his head. What were the girls thinking?

In a few minutes the two roommates returned with faces scrubbed clean and shiny. Tie Li grinned broadly, showing off her teeth. "What do you think? Look any whiter?"

Tony squinted. "Amazing," he gasped. "I've never seen such white teeth in all my life. Not in 6,000 years of history has any 12-year-old owned a more perfect, more brilliant set of grinders. You've broken all records for whiteness and mouth appeal."

Tie Li turned to her friend. "My brother tends to over-exaggerate from time to time. Ignore him."

Olena grinned. "Oh, I do. Every day."

"Hey," Tony countered, "after seeing you both a few minutes ago, anything looks beautiful."

"Olena!" Mrs. Parks' voice rang out from the doorway. "Social Services wants to talk to you." She handed the girl the cordless phone.

The person on the other end of the line spoke for a few moments. Then the color drained from Olena's face. Handing the phone back to Mrs. Parks, she said quietly, "Now they want to talk to you."

Mrs. Parks left the room with the receiver pressed against her ear.

"What's wrong?" Tie Li asked.

"My mother is . . . in jail. Somewhere in Texas."

"Jail? In Texas?" repeated Tony, remembering the e-mail message he'd received from Dark Angel.

"She was arrested yesterday with some illegal drugs in her possession. Not a whole lot, you understand. The police said she wasn't trying to sell them, just use them, I guess."

"I'm really sorry," Tony said, lifting his hands in a helpless gesture.

"My mother is not exactly what you'd call strong. She can be talked into almost anything. Someone got her hooked, and now she's an addict."

"No," said Mrs. Parks as she returned to the room. "They did a blood test, and it revealed no traces of contraband in her body. But there were signs of alcohol in her bloodstream."

Olena glanced at her companions. "She's really a nice person," she said. "Mother took good care of me, even when my father was—" Her words slipped into silence. After a moment, she continued. "I'm scared for my mom— and I miss her. I miss her voice talking to me and how she breathed so softly as she slept beside me at night."

There was silence in the room for a long moment, then Olena looked at Mrs. Parks. "When mom and dad separated, Mother told me that she and I would stay together and not let anything tear us apart. She said we'd survive no matter what. I believed her. Now I don't know what to believe."

Tony swallowed hard. "I'm sorry," he said, glancing at

his own mother who had wrapped loving arms around Olena. Tie Li was crying softly. "I'm really sorry," Tony said again. He turned to go, then hesitated. "I'm sure she loves you very much."

"Then why did she leave?" Olena asked, suddenly angry.

The boy shook his head. "Even my computer can't answer that kind of question. It can only show stuff based on facts—it can't read minds. Sometimes I wish it could," he said wistfully.

"Thanks, Tony," Olena replied with a tired smile. "You're a true friend, all of you."

As Tony and Mrs. Parks left the room the girl stood and moved to the window. "Have you ever had someone you love walk out on you?" she asked Tie Li.

Her friend nodded. "Sorta. My brother Kim. When I found out that he had survived the fire in my village, I was so happy. But his mind had gotten hurt by the war. It took him a long time to learn how to act like my brother again. He used to pretend that I didn't exist."

"What did you do?"

"I learned that I had to love him, even when he did things that hurt my feelings and made me cry." The girl brightened. "Now he's away at a private school and writes to me every week."

"And you're not angry about what happened?"

"Not anymore. I'd rather miss my brother than be angry at him."

Olena nodded. "Who taught you how to love like that?"

"Someone who said we should love people even when they don't love us," Tie Li said softly.

The young Russian sighed. "He sounds nice."
Tie Li nodded her head. "Yes. He was."

As night gripped the city in an icy sleep, a computer program stirred at a preset hour, bringing itself to life deep within the confines of a device attached to the Internet. In seconds it was streaming along global communication lines, searching for information about prisons and about a certain man who saw into the future. Tony figured it was time for Olena to find some answers too.

The elevated train swayed back and forth as it rumbled through the towering skyscrapers of downtown Chicago. Tony sat with his nose buried in a computer magazine as Tie Li and Olena watched glass-and-concrete offices rush by.

It had been a week and a half since the Parks family had welcomed the strange visitor into their home, and already she seemed part of the family. Olena had registered for classes at the same school where her two young friends attended.

Their days had fallen into a predictable pattern: a hurried breakfast, a hurried run to the train station, hurried studies, hurried classes, and in the middle of it all, a hurried lunch.

Now the three weary young people could catch their breath. They were looking forward to the more relaxed pace of the afternoon and evening hours to come.

Suddenly scowling faces appeared hovering over the seat in front of them. "Hey, Russian," a teenager sneered. "I hear your mom's in the slammer."

Olena turned sharply toward Tony, who frowned and shook his head, indicating that he hadn't said anything to anyone.

"Yeah," the other boy pressed, "we overheard a teacher talking to the vice-principal about this foreign woman whose daughter's at our school. They were wondering what they should do, you know, whether they should throw you in with her in case you've got the same criminal genes as she has, or if they should just throw you out onto the street where you belong."

Tony's eyes narrowed. "Cool it, Mason. Olena's mom is none of your business!"

"Hey," the bully countered, "I'm just trying to protect myself. I mean, if this illegal alien is a threat to my security, I wanna know. Can't be too careful about criminals from Russia. I hear they're real monsters."

Olena burst out of her seat and yanked the speaker up, almost slamming his head into the overhanging coat rack. "My mother is not a criminal!" the girl said through clenched teeth. "She just can't get enough to eat. Do you know what that is like?"

The boy shook his head, his cheeks as white as the snow falling outside.

"She doesn't have a job," Olena continued, "which means she can't buy herself a half-decent coat to wear. Have you ever been really cold and can't do anything about it?"

Again the boy shook his head no.

"My mother trusts people," Olena said, pushing her face close to the boy's. "But they keep getting her into trouble, and she ends up in jail while those she trusted run away like scared dogs. Before you call anyone a criminal, I suggest you know the facts. Then try showing some compassion." With that she dropped the teenager from her grip.

Olena sat down and turned to her companions, who were staring at her, mouths open. The girl smiled sweetly. "I'm hungry," she said. "Do you have any fruit left from lunch?"

Tie Li fished around in her backpack, eyes still fixed on Olena. She withdrew a shiny red apple. Olena accepted it and sat back to enjoy her snack. The boy who'd been seated in front of them, along with a buddy, stood up and found a new seat elsewhere.

Tony grinned. "Olena, I hope those guys didn't, uh, frighten you."

The girl shrugged. "I think we understand each other now."

The swaying train continued its journey into the city.

"Where are we going?" Olena asked as Tony led her and Tie Li through the lobby of the tall office building where Mr. Parks worked.

Tony smiled. "You'll see."

Earlier, after telling his parents that he and the girls were going to spend the evening doing computer stuff, the three had left the apartment and hurried along the cold, busy street to company headquarters two blocks away.

The lobby was emptying fast as workers headed home. Entering the elevator, Tony instructed it to travel to level 36, one floor higher than it usually rose. Olena just stood and watched the flickering lights indicate each passing level as they ascended higher and higher.

Olena frowned. "What's up here?" she asked.

The boy smiled over at his sister. "Well, I call it VR-2002. Neat name, huh?"

The girl shook her head. She had no idea what Tony was talking about most of the time. Why should this evening be any different?

As the elevator bumped to a stop and the door slid open, Olena knew her friend had totally lost his marbles. "There's nothing out here but an unfinished floor!" Olena stated, mystified.

"Wait," Tie Li encouraged. "It gets better."

"What are those?" Olena asked, motioning toward several machines positioned along the distant walls more than 100 feet away.

Tony waved for the two girls to follow. He spoke as they walked along the uncarpeted floor. "You see, Olena, Tie Li and I like to find out about the past—I mean the real, long-forgotten, history-books past. I once built a machine that, well, showed us what life was like many, *many* years ago. But, it was destroyed in the storm that leveled our farm. So I've made another machine, or a group of machines, that can do sorta the same thing. Only this time we'll be seeing scenes created in *virtual* reality—you

know, computer-generated images projected in three dimensions into empty space."

Olena stopped. "I don't understand."

Tony smiled patiently. "Have you ever seen a hologram?"

"A holo—what?"

"Hologram. You know, a picture of something, but it
looks real, kinda floating in space."

"Oh, yes," Olena breathed. "I saw one at the science
museum."

"Well, I can generate holograms of big things: trees,
mountains, rocks, and—" he hesitated, "and people."

"People?"

"Yes. They can move around and even talk, if I have
the right data fed into the computer."

"Wow! You can do all that?"

"Yes, with the help of a whole bunch of computers and
other equipment." The boy ran to a set of keyboards
mounted by a wall. "Here, I'll show you."

He entered a command. Suddenly the lights in the room
flickered off, leaving a strange glow pulsating near the center of the large expanse. "Are you watching?" Tony called.

"Yes," came the somewhat uncertain reply from the
distant shadows.

"OK. Here goes." Olena saw Tony place some sort of
small metal box near his lips. "SIMON, run exterior portion
of simulation A40, half effects, quarter processing power."

"SIMON running simulation as requested," a metallic
voice announced.

Suddenly a full-grown tree appeared, spreading lush
green leaves out over the floor, stretching high into what

looked to be an empty, cloudless sky.

Olena backed away in breathless wonder. "Th-that's impossible!"

"No," Tony called. "That's virtual reality!"

The girl circled the tree, staring up into its perfectly represented branches, her mouth agape. "How?" she asked.

"Lots of processing power. But never mind all that right now. I want to do something for you. You mentioned a few days ago you wished you knew more about where your mom is at."

"You mean—"

"That's right, Olena. I want to take you there."

CHAPTER 06

PRISON VISIT

Come over here," Tony called, motioning toward one side of the large expanse.

Olena glanced up at the virtual tree already being projected and frowned. "Is it going to hurt?"

"No," the boy chuckled. "Using data from a whole bunch of sources, we'll look at the virtual image of the prison where they're holding your mom."

Suddenly rough block walls rose from the floor. They saw a shiny tile hallway dimly lit by bare bulbs hanging from the ceiling. A jail cell at the far end of the passageway looked as though it hadn't been painted for years.

Olena glanced at Tony and Tie Li, her eyes filled with uncertainty. The boy smiled and asked, "Do you want to continue?"

"Yes," came the quiet reply.

Tony entered another command on his keyboard. "Almost there," he whispered. "Just a little more magnification."

It seemed as though the three young people were moving down a long hallway and then into a prison cell. In the dim light they saw the foot of a steel bunk. A solitary sink and toilet bowl were the only other pieces of "furniture" within the enclosure.

Olena stared at the images, her heart breaking. So this was what it looked like, what awaited someone who lived by the empty promises of people who didn't care. The girl glanced away. She knew that her mother had been searching for love and acceptance in the wrong places—at smoke-filled bars and on the streets. The men she'd met would woo her with sugary talk and exciting promises. For some reason she'd believed them. Now they were gone.

"My mother never liked it when I said that the men she ran around with weren't good for her. She must have gotten tired of hearing me say those things. I just wanted her to be happy. I didn't mean to chase her away."

Olena covered her face with her hands and sobbed.

"Olena?" Tony said. "I didn't mean for this to hurt you. Do you want me to switch it off?"

The teen lowered her fingers and looked at him. "All my mother ever wanted was a home," she said, "a place where people would care for her, where she could feel safe." She turned toward Tie Li. "Was that too much to ask?"

The girl looked at Tony for an answer.

Tony shook his head. "Tie Li and I learned that's what the Creator-God wanted when He made this earth. He wanted us to be happy."

"Creator-God?"

"You see," Tie Li joined in, "that Man I told you about— the One who helped me learn to forgive—His name is Jesus. He is also the Creator-God. He created the world and the whole universe. But then Satan showed up, and people chose to follow him. They started hurting each other, fighting wars, worshiping things like statues and stars."

"Satan?" Olena blinked, confused. "Who's Satan?"

"He's the devil—the enemy of God," explained Tie Li. "He used to be one of the beautiful angels God created. His name was Lucifer. He got jealous because everyone worshiped the Creator-God instead of him. So he started a rebellion and convinced many angels to join his side. But God threw Lucifer out of heaven. That's how he ended up on this earth, causing trouble for people like us—like your mother."

Tony nodded in agreement. "God the Father and the Creator-God made a plan to save people from Satan. The plan was for Jesus to come to this earth and pay the penalty for all the sins Satan led them to commit. But when Jesus was born as a human being, few people paid any attention to what He said. He promised that a new world would come for those who believed in Him and obeyed His words, but a lot of people—even the rulers— laughed and said He was crazy. And one terrible afternoon, an angry mob had Him killed. But He rose up out of His grave and returned to heaven."

"Wait!" Olena called out, waving her hand. "This is all new to me. I don't understand."

Tie Li touched her arm. "It's a beautiful story, really," she said softly.

Tony stepped forward and held Olena's gaze with his. "We want to understand what's been happening since Jesus went back to heaven. Some people believed in Him and obeyed the instructions He left behind. But a lot of people quit believing. Tie Li and I want to know why. We want to know how the story ends."

"Yes," Tie Li agreed. "We want to understand about all the bad things that happen in this world. So Tony is going to help us look into the past with his computers." She paused. "Olena, since you're our 'sister' for a little while, we thought you might like to find some answers with us."

The Russian thought for a moment. "If there's a new world coming, a place where there's no sadness or pain, I want to know about it too. Yes. Let me search with you."

The boy nodded. "Some of the historical simulations may be kinda rough," he warned. "The past hasn't always been pleasant."

"Neither is life," the girl said without emotion.

Tony nodded in agreement, then tapped on the keyboard.

Olena saw the image of the prison fade from view. Then she watched as Tony lifted a small metal box to his lips and speak slowly and clearly. "SIMON, begin simulation A41, full effects, 100 percent processing power."

In an instant, their drab surroundings were transformed into a windblown mountaintop where gnarled scrub trees clung to jagged rocks. Distant gulls floated on the breeze as their cry echoed off the cliffs. Olena was about to call out in surprise when a sound caught the young people's attention. Turning, they noticed an old man kneeling in a sheltered spot by the crest of the cliff overlooking the shore. His white hair and beard trailed in the wind like tattered flags.

Tie Li moved forward. "Why, Tony?" she called over her shoulder. "Why is this old man crying?"

The boy glanced across the expanse of sky and sea. Far below, virtual breakers washed over a rocky beach, sending shorebirds scurrying. "He's a prisoner here," Tony responded. "They exiled him to this island to die."

"Who exiled him?" Olena asked.

"The same people who killed another Man we once saw," came the somber reply. "The man's name was Paul. Those people didn't want either Paul or this Man to talk about Jesus, the Creator and Son of God. But a Book I have says that something wonderful happened on this island."

"What?"

Tony glanced over at the man. "He . . . he dreamed."

Suddenly a streak of light split the sky and sped past the mountaintop, shaking the ground with its passing. The very air seemed to become static with energy. The three youngsters fell back in fright, hiding their faces from the brilliance. Then all was calm.

"What was that?" Tie Li gasped.

Tony didn't answer. He stood still, staring up into the heavens. When Tie Li and Olena glanced in the same direction, their breath caught in their throats. Hovering not more than 100 feet away was a shimmering being, tall and proud, held aloft by unseen wings, surrounded by a silver light that seemed to shine from inside his body.

The old man stumbled to his feet and turned to face the shining being. "What is it?" he called out, his voice trembling. "What do you want to tell me?"

The shimmering being lifted its hands to its mouth and called out in a clear, powerful voice, "Love God. Glorify Him because He has come to judge the earth. Worship Him who made everything!"

Just as the speaker finished, another bolt of energy swept over the mountaintop, shaking the ground and causing Tony and the others to stumble back in astonishment. It too paused in midair, forming another being bathed in brilliant light and floating like the first.

"Fallen!" the second speaker shouted in an excited voice. "Fallen is Babylon the great, which made all nations sin against God!"

As this being finished delivering its message, another presence swept past, splitting the sky with its movement. Exactly as those before it, the newcomer stopped and lifted its hands to its mouth and shouted: "If anyone believes the beast and thinks or acts like it, he will know God's fury! He will die in the presence of all things holy and will be no more forever. But God's people must remain faithful to heaven's commandments of love. They must be patient . . . patient . . . patient!" The words echoed across the island like thunder.

After the beings vanished, the sky returned to its normal blue and the sound of gulls rose again from the distant shore.

Olena's hand trembled as she held Tony's arm for support. She continued to gaze at the spot in the sky where the beings had appeared moments before.

Tie Li fought for breath, realizing that she'd been unconsciously holding hers. "What were they?" she cried out.

"What happened?" Olena added. "It was the most scary thing I've ever seen!"

Tony, himself shaken by the sight, walked on rubbery legs a few paces forward. "Look," he called out. "Look at the old man."

The three young visitors saw the gentleman was sitting with head bent low, hand guiding a feathered quill over a piece of parchment. The scene he'd just witnessed had shaken him out of his sadness, and he wrote quickly, mumbling to himself, stopping occasionally to glance skyward before continuing his frantic scribbling.

"His name is John," Tony announced. "He was one of Jesus' disciples who received the power of the Holy Spirit to go out and preach and keep alive the work and the memory of Jesus."

"But why is he on this bare island?" Olena wanted to know.

"He was exiled by those who allowed themselves to be controlled by Satan. God gave John many dreams or visions, like the one we just saw. John met beasts and angels, horses and dragons, and heard trumpets. What he saw represented centuries of time, stretching all the way to our day—and beyond."

Olena frowned. "What did the dreams mean?"

"It's kinda complicated," Tony responded. "But I think this one, the one we just saw, might mean something important *to us* if we continue to look at history carefully."

The old man stood to his feet and started walking along the path leading down from the mountaintop.

"He wrote about the new earth," Tony said, watching him go. "He saw it in dreams and said it was very, very beautiful. I thought about trying to simulate it, but discovered it would take more power and memory than I have available. Guess we'll just have to use our imaginations."

Tony lifted the device out in front of him. "SIMON," he commanded. "Set defaults and end simulation. Realign buffers for normal operation. Store dream sequence for later review."

The mountaintop vanished, leaving the young people standing alone in the vast emptiness of the unfinished thirty-sixth floor of the office building. Around them, machines clicked and snapped as processors and projectors cooled.

Olena stood lost in thought. "This Jesus you talk about—He made the dreams the old man saw?"

"Yes," Tony said, checking a case of components.

"Then He should know what He's talking about," the girl stated.

"Yeah? Why?"

"Because if He created everything, He should know how to re-create it, right?"

Tie Li nodded. "That makes sense to me. Now, we just have to figure out what the three messages meant. The first being said something about God judging the earth. The second being shouted that Babylon—whatever that is—is fallen. And then the third said we should worship God so we won't be destroyed forever."

"And we gotta have patience," Tony added. Then he frowned. "Patience for what?"

Olena shook her head. "All this stuff is going to make my brain melt right out of my ears. Come on, Tie Li. Let's get back to the apartment before Tony takes us somewhere else that scares us to death."

The boy laughed and headed for the elevator. "OK, you guys. I'll take it a little easier from now on. I promise. No more bright beings flying around the sky."

"Where are we going next time?" Tie Li wanted to know.

The boy grinned. "You may not like my choice of destinations."

"Oh?" Olena said. "Where are we headed, to another island where some of those beasts you mentioned are running around?"

Tony shook his head. "Not exactly. But we might meet some pretty bad dudes."

"So," his sister urged, "where are you taking us?"

The boy hesitated, then said, "Rome."

Tie Li gasped. Why would Tony want to take them to the very city where one man lost his head and another got banished forever to a place of wild and frightening dreams?

Tony couldn't sleep. He just lay in his bed staring at the designs on his bedroom curtains. Most evenings he'd drift into dreamland the moment his head hit the pillow, but not tonight. Instead of the usual soothing visions of computer chips and high-speed processors, one image seemed to be burned into his consciousness. It was that third being, hovering with the others above the island, shouting out its message, warning of a beast that no one should worship. A beast! Who in their right mind would worship a beast?

The boy frowned. In their journeys in *Voyager,* Tie Li and he had seen people worshiping in gardens, churches, and temples. But *nowhere* had there been a beast wandering about insisting that folks bow down to it. Besides that, what did this beast have to do with the new earth Jesus had promised?

Tony slipped from beneath the covers and stumbled through the darkness to his desk. He flopped down in his chair and stared at the silent computer screen in front of him. Then, with a giant chest-expanding yawn, he reached out and flipped on the CPU. In glowing red letters it invited, "Enter your command:"

Tony yawned again. "SIMON," he said.

Within seconds a voice rattled from the device resting by the computer. "SIMON standing by."

"SIMON, define the word 'beast' as used in the Book I downloaded into your memory before we started the simulations."

The little screen on the device flickered to life, scrolling through entries as SIMON scanned the Book from beginning to end.

Then the light faded. "Task completed," SIMON said.

"Report."

"The Book uses the word *beast* to represent animals, some clean, some unclean, some used for offerings or sacrifices, some—"

"SIMON," Tony interrupted, "when is a beast *not* a beast?"

SIMON's lights flickered as the unit searched for the answer to Tony's unusual question.

CHAPTER 07

POWER STRUGGLE

Tony repeated his question, trying to phrase it more clearly. "SIMON, when does the Book use the word *beast* to mean something other than an animal? Cross-reference message of the third being from our last situation."

SIMON's screen flickered to life once again as it scanned through the volume stored in its memory. Then the light dimmed.

"A beast is not a beast when it is a power," the device stated.

"A power?"

"Yes. The Book says there is one beast that does something nonstandard."

"What?"

"Change the law."

Tony frowned. *"What* law?"

SIMON clicked a few times as if checking its facts. Then it answered. "The law of God."

The boy stared at the device. Change God's law? That was impossible! That law was responsible for every detail in the world of science. It kept planets in orbit, drove seasons across the face of nature, organized molecules into trees, oceans, and aardvarks.

"Are you sure?" Tony asked.

SIMON answered without hesitation. "Yes."

As he turned off his computer, Tony stared into the darkness. This was one of the most incredible things he'd ever heard! Somewhere, hidden in the past, was a power that changed God's law. Most amazing of all, apparently there were people willing to *worship* this beast!

As he returned to his bed, a new thought came to Tony's tired mind. As incredible as it sounded, the being in John's vision had stated that before anyone could enjoy the new home Jesus had promised, they'd have to face the beast.

Olena wrinkled her nose. "Hold on a minute," she said as she and Tie Li waited for the elevator to reach the office building's thirty-sixth floor. "Are you saying that this world exists because the Creator-God *told* it to?"

Tie Li nodded. "Yes. He just spoke and everything . . . well . . . appeared. Birds, fish, mountains, even people. First they weren't, then they were. Neat, huh?"

The Russian girl blinked. *"People?"* The science textbooks I've read in school said we came from monkeys."

"No, Olena. Everything in the universe came directly from the hand of God. *Everything*—even Tony, although he sometimes *acts* as if he's part monkey."

"I heard that," Tony called from across the room as the elevator doors rolled open.

Olena giggled. "I did notice that he put an extra helping of bananas on his breakfast cereal this morning."

"I'm not a monkey," the boy insisted as the girls joined him by a stack of equipment. "I'm a human being who happens to like bananas." He peered into the innards of a computer case. "Hand me that little wrench over there, would you?"

Tie Li followed her brother's waving finger and found the tool. "This one?"

"Yeah. Thanks."

As she handed the tool to her brother, she burst out laughing. "What's so funny?" Tony wanted to know.

"That tool," Tie Li giggled. "It's a *monkey* wrench."

Olena laughed too, causing Tony to blush crimson.

"I should send you two to the top of a virtual volcano, but I won't. Instead, we're going to meet a guy who did something kind of impossible."

"What?"

"You'll see."

Tony lifted his ever-present device to his lips. "SIMON, begin simulation A41, full effects and processing power."

"Simulation under way," the metallic voice responded.

Suddenly the three found themselves standing near the balcony of a large stone building overlooking a vast throng of people. In the distance the pillars of other structures rose majestically into the warm sunshine and blue canopy sky.

Colorful flags fluttered in the breezes, but the people remained motionless, as if waiting for something to happen. The whole scene was one of expectation and awe.

"This is Rome, right?" Tie Li asked, remembering what her brother had said the evening before.

"Yes, in the year A.D. 321. That's almost 300 years after Jesus died."

"What are all these people waiting for?" Olena asked, motioning at the hushed multitudes spread out below.

"Their emperor is about to make a proclamation," Tony stated. "His name is Constantine, and he has this big dream of bringing all the people in his kingdom together so they can live more peacefully."

"He sounds like a good man," Tie Li said with a smile.

"You'd think so," her brother agreed, "except for how he plans to do it."

Just then the curtains hanging nearby parted and out stepped a large handsome man wearing flowing silk robes and carrying a jewel-studded staff. Encircling his head was a wreath of golden leaves.

The throng roared their welcome, shouting earthshaking greetings to the man waving down at them.

"My people, *my people!*" the man called back. "You are so generous with your praise!"

Olena smiled. "They really like him, although he could use a good hair stylist."

Tony chuckled, then lifted his hand. "Listen."

"People of Rome," the emperor shouted as the assembly ceased their wild welcome and hushed in respectful silence. "Listen to what your emperor says this day. Listen and obey." The speaker held out a parchment containing neat rows of carefully printed words. "In order to bring unity to the kingdom and assure harmony among the heathen and Christian subjects among us, let all the judges and towns people, and the occupation of all trades, rest on the venerable day of the sun." He lowered the parchment. "Your emperor has spoken. It is now so."

Wild cheers echoed again throughout the assembly as the man on the balcony waved and smiled broadly down on his subjects. Then he turned and walked back through the curtains, leaving the children alone to listen to the roar of approval.

Tie Li stared unmoving at the people. "Tony," she called, trying to be heard above the cheering, "did he say the say of the sun?"

"Yes."

Olena frowned. "What does all this mean?"

Tony lifted the device to his lips. "SIMON, mute audio."

The tumultuous shouts faded, leaving the frenzied throng below moving in complete silence. "You see," the boy stated, "Emperor Constantine told everyone to worship on the day of the sun. That was already a special day for his heathen subjects. And Christians knew that Jesus rose from the dead on that day. So both groups were given a day of worship that could be shared; Sunday."

"Was this bad?" Olena asked.

Tie Li turned to face her friend. "*Very* bad," she said. "You see, when the Creator-God made the earth, He said that the *seventh* day should be the day of worship. It was a way for everyone to remember Creation and where they came from. It was the way God asked us to honor and worship Him. He even put that law into His Ten Commandments.

Tony nodded. "What Constantine did was to try to change a law made by God."

Olena lifted her hands. "Isn't God all-powerful?" she asked. "Who would change a law made by the very God who created everything in the universe?"

Tony looked out over the city. "Not *who*," he breathed. *"What."*

Tie li blinked. "Wasn't Constantine just a man?"

"Yes," the boy stated, watching the cheering people below. "But the kingdom and belief system he stood for represented something else, something much more dangerous."

"What?"

Tony studied the marble columns and stately buildings fronting the crowded streets. Towering monuments and grim-faced statues hovered over the silent crowd as they continued their jubilant response to their leader's words. The boy shook his head slowly. "The being on the mountaintop had a word for it," he said. "He called it *the beast.*

Tie Li wrinkled her nose. "It's not going to happen."

Olena pointed as she narrowed her eyes. "I thought I saw some action on the right side."

"You guys are imagining things," Tony stated with a chuckle. "We've been here for 10 minutes, and that egg looks just as it did when we arrived."

Behind the three friends who stood huddled over a warm metal-and-glass incubator, crowds of visitors flowed past displays of military aircraft, farm machinery, old automobiles, and a miniature fairy castle. In the distance children shouted to one another, music mingled with ceaseless waves of voices, and a loudspeaker announced that someone by the name of Jessica had misplaced her mother. To anyone living in Chicago, such sounds were part of countless Sunday afternoons spent at the Museum of Science and Industry in Jackson Park.

"There!" Tie Li announced excitedly. "It's coming out. I'm sure of it."

Three faces pressed close to the glass. Three sets of eyes peered intently at the little egg now rocking gently on its soft bed of straw.

"You're right," Tony breathed. "And it's an energetic little guy, too."

A tiny crack appeared at the side of the egg, followed by a determined yellow bill. The fracture began to grow wider and wider as the chick inside fought its way into the world. In a matter of minutes a new life stumbled to its feet and staggered around the broken remnants of its shell as if to say, "OK. I'm out. Now what am I supposed to do?"

"Yes!" Olena shouted. "It made it! Oh, how cute!"

Tie Li nodded, a big smile creasing her young face. "I've seen this lots of times, but it's fun to watch again and again, even if the chick is being hatched here in this museum instead of out on our farm. Remember, Tony? Remember all the little chicks by the barn?"

"Yes," the boy nodded. "Didn't need an incubator there. Had lots of mama hens to keep things warm."

The three gazed at the new life and sighed nearly in

unison. Even in the city it was still possible to catch a glimpse of what life was like in the country, far from the noise and pollution of the modern world.

"Tony?" Olena asked as the trio walked to a bench and sat down below the wings of a jet airplane. "Tell me again what you meant when you said that Constantine was part of a beast."

The boy frowned, an expression he often formed when thinking deeply. "He and his new law were part of a 'beastly' *system.* God had told everyone to worship Him on a certain day. Constantine said, 'Forget that. Everyone should worship on the day I choose.' And he backed up his decree with violence. If you didn't do what he said, you got tossed in jail or even killed. In other words, the emperor was trying to change God's law. The Book says that any power that does this is called 'the beast.'"

"So," Tie Li interjected, "when that bright being on the mountaintop in John's vision said we shouldn't worship the beast, it was saying we shouldn't obey anyone or anything that tries to change God's law, right?"

"That's the way I see it," Tony stated.

Olena was silent for a moment. "So from then on everyone forgot about Jesus and what He said we should do and, instead, did what the beast told them to do?"

Tony lifted his hand. "I've got SIMON working on our next simulation. It should be ready tonight. Wanna see how history answers your question?"

"Sure," Olena nodded. "Jesus promised a new earth. That sounds much better than what any man or any beast can come up with."

Tie Li nodded her agreement.

After the three finished their visit to the museum with a trip through a reconstructed coal mine, complete with a little train rumbling through deep, dark tunnels, they hopped onto a crowded bus and rode back to the heart of the city. As late afternoon rays from the sun slipped between the towering buildings, they saw many churches along the way. Tony noticed that not one of them announced that sacred services were scheduled on the day God had decreed was His choice for worship.

At the apartment the three young people enjoyed steaming-hot bowls of tomato soup and the rich flavor of homemade wheat bread piled high with lettuce, tomato slices, and chunks of green pepper. Afterward they excused themselves and hurried to the office building. They were eager to experience another virtual visit to the past. More important, they wanted the answer to a question that now burned in their thoughts: Had the beast won?

Tony nodded to himself as he studied the screen of a computer mounted against the far wall of the empty thirty-sixth floor. "Yes! SIMON has finished our research," he called to his companions. "We've got another sim ready to go."

"What will we see?" Tie Li asked.

"Not what—*who,*" the boy stated, tapping lightly on a keyboard. "SIMON found a man who did something very amazing."

"Did he see bright beings in the sky?" Olena wanted to know.

The boy read the writing on the screen. "No. But this

man *was* on an island. This time it was just off the north-western coast of Scotland, in the year A.D. 563." Tony entered one more command, then lifted the device to his lips, "SIMON, create simulation A42, full effects and power." He turned to his two companions standing not far away. "You guys might want to move a little to the left."

Tie Li and Olena shrugged and obeyed. Just as they shifted position, a large stone wall appeared where they'd been standing. Turning around, they jumped when they saw a powerfully built man guiding a wooden wheelbarrel in their direction. Nearby two other workers hauled large cut stones on their backs.

Voices shouted from every direction, calling for more mortar, more sand, and new jugs of water.

"What's going on?" Tie Li asked, hurrying to her brother's side. Olena followed close behind.

"It's a Christian monastery," Tony responded, sweeping his hand over his head, admiring the rising structure.

"A monastery for what?" Tie Li asked as yet another construction worker stumbled past.

Tony led the girls to another vantage point, passing virtual walls and stone-littered roadways en route. When they finally halted, they stood where a green lawn swept majestically down a hill and ended at the edge of a sparkling ocean.

With the sounds of hammering and shouting now dulled by distance, they heard a male voice calling out from below. Following the words, they saw a gathering of people seated comfortably by the waters.

"I tell you a mystery," the speaker was saying, his hand waving out in front of him as if parting unseen curtains.

"There is a power stronger than any earthly power. It is centered in the life of Jesus Christ, the Saviour of humankind."

"Who is he?" Olena asked, finding herself drawn to the kind eyes and sincere manner of the preacher. The man wore a simple brown robe tied at the waist with a rope. His face was clean-shaven and ruddy, weathered by years of wind and sun.

Tony checked the little scene on the device. "That, my friends, is a man about to challenge the beast."

CHAPTER 08

THE COURAGE OF COLUMBA

Tony, Tie Li, and Olena stood spellbound as the man by the shore spoke. His audience, so realistically portrayed by Tony's powerful projectors, were dressed in handmade farmer's clothes and sat in hushed silence, drinking in every word.

"There was a man, a bishop in the early Christian church," the monk said as he searched the faces of his listeners, "who dared stand against the laws of earthly powers. When Roman rulers instructed him to say 'Caesar is Lord,' he refused. Three times they demanded that he utter those words. And three times Bishop Polycarp remained mute. He knew there was only one true Lord, and that was Jesus Christ. So on a terrible day in A.D. 155 an angry mob turned on him, stabbed the life from his body, and burned his corpse to ashes. Polycarp, like John the Revelator, stood firm in his convictions, even if it meant giving up life itself."

The man paused and stared up at the uncompleted monastery rising above them on the crest of the hill. "I am building a house of God on this island, a place where champions of truth will be honored, not persecuted. Jesus accepted His destiny by being born as a baby in Bethlehem and living a life free from sin. Now it is your turn. You can be part of that same destiny. You can live the truth and die the truth."

The speaker moved closer to his hearers. "Friends," he said, his voice filled with emotion, "that truth is found in history, not in the laws of human beings. It was planted in Eden by God Himself and can now grow in your hearts."

"Of what truth do you speak, Columba?" a member of the audience called out respectfully. "You taught us of a Saviour who can forgive our sins. You've shown us that we can pray directly to Him without having to depend on other human beings to speak our words for us. What else do we need to know?"

Tony leaned close to Tie Li. "Here it comes," he whispered.

Columba smiled as a breeze ruffled his robe. "There is a day unlike any other in the week, a day set aside for worship."

"We keep the Sabbath," someone called from the gathering.

"No!" Columba retorted. "You keep a false Sabbath, a day decreed by human beings. I speak of a more noble selection, a Sabbath fashioned by God Himself. It was set apart on the seventh day of Creation week and made holy by Him. *This* is the day that seals your destiny. *This* is the day of *truth!*"

Tie Li gasped. "Tony. *Tony!*" she whispered, barely able to hold back her excitement. "That's the *Creation* Sabbath he's talking about. Constantine didn't change God's law! He couldn't. People still believed. People still trusted in what Jesus taught!"

Olena frowned slightly. "This is good, right?"

"This is very good," Tony stated. "We now know that in the sixth century after Christ, some people still stood up to the beast." The boy pointed at the preacher who continued to address his audience. "That monk, Columba, finished his monastery and made this tiny island of Iona a sort of evangelistic center. He opened a school and sent out missionaries not only to Scotland and England, but to Germany, Switzerland, and even Rome itself. Because of him and his followers, the Creation Sabbath and memories of Jesus' promises were kept alive. For centuries the beast was challenged. But . . ."

Tie Li noticed that her brother's smile had faded. "But what, Tony?"

The boy lifted the device to his lips. "SIMON, end simulation."

As the scene faded, leaving the trio standing alone in the empty space that had moments before been a beautiful landscape filled with trees and edged by ocean waves, Tony sighed a deep, troubled sigh. "My research shows that there were dark days ahead for those who stood against the beast."

Tie Li frowned. "Was it bad?"

"Yes," her brother nodded. "Very bad."

"But," Olena interjected, "at least we're learning the truth, right? This proves that the idea of a new earth is still true, right?"

"Seems so," Tony agreed, "but a lot of people suffered terribly holding on to that dream."

"Suffered? How?" Tie Li asked.

"You don't want to know," the boy said. "Trust me, little sister, you don't want to know."

After the girls returned home, Tony sat alone beside the main processor in his large VR-2002 room. He listened as the slowly cooling projectors clicked and snapped, as the hard drive in his computer whirled, processing new streams of information being fed to it from the Internet by the software application he called SIMON.

The machines were operating exactly as Tony had planned, recreating scenes in virtual reality from the past based on bits and pieces of information he'd collected from around the world.

But the boy was concerned. What is, after they'd finished their searches, after all the data was in, after they'd assembled and digested every piece of information that existed concerning past generations' acceptance or rejection of the truth, what if the result made it clear that the beast had won?

Columba had told his listeners by the sea that there had been champions of truth ever since Christ had died, men and women who had remained firm in what they believed no matter what.

He'd already researched what historians called the Dark Ages, when spiritual and governmental leaders did horrible things to those who stood firm in their faith. The detailed description of torment and death he'd found had made him sick to his stomach. An uneasy feeling crept into his body as he waited for SIMON to complete its latest tasks. Had all the champions died? Had truth been burned up, ripped apart, hung on crosses, or sacrificed along with those who held it dear?

A soft beep jolted the boy's thoughts to the present. He glanced down at the screen and noticed that the little mailbox symbol was flashing.

"I don't want to talk to you," he said out loud, knowing full well who had sent the unread message.

The box blinked on and off, on and off.

"Who are you?" the boy asked softly. "How do you track me so well? How do you always seem to know what I'm doing?"

The little symbol continued to blink, waiting for a response.

Tony reached over and took hold of the computer mouse. He moved the cursor to the box and, with a sigh, clicked once.

A little window opened on the screen.

"Greetings, Tony Parks. There's nothing in the past worth finding. The more you look, the more hate you'll uncover." It was signed "Dark Angel."

After reading the note, the boy noticed that the reply symbol was illuminated. He gasped. That meant that whoever had sent the message was still online, still connected, waiting for a response in real time. This had never happened before with this sender.

Tony grabbed his device and jammed it to his lap. "SIMON," he called, "stop processing incoming data and trace all e-mail and chat connections to unit three. NOW!"

"SIMON tracing real-time data stream as requested," a metalic voice announced without hesitation.

The boy clicked on the reply symbol and centered his fingers above the keyboard. Whoever this Dark Angel character was, he or she was about to begin a conversation with someone who planned to find out, once and for all, their true identity. Tony knew it wouldn't be easy. Dark Angel was smart, but was he or she crafty enough to hide from the probing power contained in an entire Chicago skyscraper?

Tony's fingers tapped heavily on the keyboard. "Who are you?" he queried, keeping an eye on another screen by his elbow as SIMON began scanning every communication link in the building as well as those connected directly to the Internet.

After a short pause, a reply scrolled into view. "Someone who thinks your search is a waste of time."

"Explain," Tony typed.

Another pause. "You're chasing fairy tales and rumors. There is no God."

"Why do you say that?" Tony asked as the keys clicked to his touch.

SIMON's lightning-speed examination of the building's routers and cables continued.

"Are you happy?" the mysterious writer wanted to know. "Do you feel safe and contented?"

Tony frowned. "It's hard to feel happy when you're someplace you don't really want to be," he responded.

"Exactly," came the quick reply. "If there was a God who loves and cares for people, do you think He'd want us living on *this* earth? Get real."

SIMON flashed numbers on its screen, narrowing the search, getting closer and closer to the electronic roots of the messages.

"But sin made what is good into something bad," Tony typed. "It changed everything."

"You're wrong," flashed the responder. "Sin is real. God is fake. There is only evil because people are evil."

"That's not true." Tony's fingers hit the keys with determination. "God originally created people to be good."

SIMON raced along, scanning the millions of possible connections within the skyscraper, methodically moving in on the link connecting Tony with his mysterious correspondent.

"You're living in a dream," the writer noted. "Wake up, Tony Parks. Wake up." Then the words "Signing off" appeared.

"No, wait!" the boy typed.

The reply symbol disappeared from the screen. Tony grabbed the device and shouted at it. "SIMON? Where did it come from? *Where?*"

The little screen's images froze in mid-process as the software crashed.

"No!" Tony moaned in anger. *"No, SIMON!* Reestablish default settings. *Reboot!"*

Nothing happened.

The boy closed his eyes in frustration. This was incredible. Whomever he'd been chatting with moments before had not only sidestepped SIMON's frantic search, but had even caused the software to crash.

Tony understood exactly how it had happened. Somewhere, hidden within the communication system, Dark Angel had planted an electronic virus that, when scanned, simply canceled the search stream and shorted out the set of chips driving SIMON's operation. A thin line of blue smoke curling from one of the device's metal seams confirmed his conclusion.

"Unbelievable!" the boy sighed through gritted teeth, picking up his treasured piece of equipment and turning it over and over in his hands. "You're good, Dark Angel," he said, "You're very good."

Popping the back of the device, Tony shook his head. "Yeah, it took out the AL-3400 chipset. Fried it like a hotcake." The boy signed again. "This character sure doesn't want to be found."

Slipping the device into his backpack, he switched off the remaining equipment positioned around the empty confines of VR-2002 and headed for the elevator. He'd replace the chips tomorrow. Right then, all he wanted to do was get home and think about anything but computers and Dark Angel. He'd leave the continuing search for answers until later.

"Well, well," Mr. Lester called out as Tony burst into the workroom. "So glad you decided to make an appearance this afternoon."

Tony smiled. "I always come here after school," he chuckled. "If I didn't, you'd have me arrested or something."

The man paused, a circuit board held tightly between his

fingers. "Now, there's a thought. I can see the headlines the next day. 'Nerd Turns Nerd in For Un-nerd-like Behavior.'"

"I'm not a nerd," Tony countered, making himself comfortable at his workstation.

"Do you love computers?"

"Sure do."

"Do you know how to fix 'em when they break?"

"Yes."

"Do you often speak in technical language while in mixed company, causing your hearers to ask 'What are you talking about?'"

The boy grinned. "I suppose so."

"Then you're a nerd," Mr. Lester stated flatly. "Get used to it."

Tony shook his head. "Well, right now I'm a nerd with a burned-out set of AL-3400s. A rogue virus cooked them during a transfer sweep on a chat frequency last night."

The man blinked. "What are you talking about?"

Tony laughed. "Very funny, Mr. Lester. You know, you're more nerd than I am!"

The boy's companion pointed in the direction of a storage cabinet. "Got some extra 3400s on the second shelf."

"You do?"

"Yeah. Use 'em on the server up on 22. They're always blowing out. You'd think the manufacturers would use better sand in their silicon. Probably just go down to the beach and scoop some up and pat it down with their fingers."

Tony chuckled at the image Mr. Lester's comment created in his mind. Silicon, the material with which manufacturers make chips, is very carefully created. Only high-grade sand is included in the process. The thought of someone just wandering down to a beach, dumping sand into a bucket, and—

The boy blinked. *Wow, I really am a nerd!* he thought. *No one else would think Mr. Lester's idea was funny!*

"So," the computer technician called to Tony, "how's your little experiment going?"

Tony shrugged. "Fine."

Mr. Lester studied the boy. "You don't seem all that thrilled."

He saw his companion shake his head. "I don't know. I've dug up some pretty nasty stuff. Seems if you believe in something, there's always someone else standing around waiting to knock you down, you know, trying to prove you wrong."

Mr. Lester brushed shiny solder shavings from his shirt. "If you ask me, it's a waste of time."

Tony glanced up from his work in surprise. "Why do you say that?"

"Most answers just raise more questions," the man remarked. "Pretty soon you're goin' around in circles. I don't like thinking that hard."

"So," Tony pressed, "you think I should stop my experiment?"

"Hey, I can't tell you what to do. I just don't think you should get your hopes up too high. You might discover things you don't like—then where would you be? You'd end up like me: mad at the world, talking to computers as if they were real people, depressing your coworker like I'm doing right now."

"You're not depressing me. Honest," Tony said. He

paused a moment and then decided to confide in Mr. Lester. "It's this Dark Angel."

"Dark Angel?"

Tony nodded. "Yeah. Someone keeps sending me messages. I don't know who he or she is, but Dark Angel seems to know everything I'm doing. It's really weird—and a little scary."

Mr. Lester picked up a screwdriver and began turning a fastener at one corner of a computer case. "Talk is cheap," he said. "I wouldn't worry about this Dark Angel."

"The person crashed my search program."

The man looked up in surprise. "That's the rogue virus you were talking about?"

"Yeah. Fried my 3400s. Pretty amazing."

Mr. Lester frowned. "I'd watch out if I were you, Tony. There's no telling what else this Dark Angel is up to. And keep in mind that even though you have permission, you're using company equipment after hours. This whole building's communication system could fry just as easy as your 3400s."

The boy nodded. "I know, but . . ." he moved closer to his friend. "I've got a plan."

"You do?" Mr. Lester breathed.

"Yeah."

"What is it?"

Tony chuckled. "Hey," he said, looking around playfully as if they were being watched. "This room might be bugged or something. Let's just say that the next time Dark Angel tries to mess with this nerd, he or she is in for a surprise."

The boy returned to his afternoon project, leaving his boss sitting quietly at his workstation.

CHAPTER 09

VOICE FROM THE DARKNESS

Traffic on Interstate 94 was light as Mr. Parks guided the family car north toward Winnetka. The Sunday afternoon sun shone bravely through the frigid air, trying its best to bring warmth to the occupants of the speeding vehicle.

Tony and Tie Li sat in the back seat, with Olena riding between them. All three were taking in the harsh winter landscape, trying to remember what the world looked like before the snow came.

"Will it ever be green again?" Tie Li asked, eyeing a small field where corn had grown. "Sometimes I think Illinois will be white forever."

"It'll be green and yellow and red," Tony enthused, trying to bolster his own doubts about the climate of his home state. "Spring's coming, I'm sure."

"I like spring," Olena interjected. "It's a new beginning, a fresh start. Birds sing, flowers grow. And stores cut prices to make room for new merchandise!"

Tony chuckled. "Someone's been watching too much TV. You sound like the guy from that clothing store in Aurora."

Tie Li nodded. "He has some pretty good deals on

flannel pajamas. I thought I'd get some for you, Tony. You'd look cute in flannel jammies."

"Forget it," the boy said, blushing. "I sleep in T-shirts and jogging shorts—I don't need anything fancy. Can we talk about something else?"

"Sure, what?"

"Anything!"

As the banter continued in the back seat, Mr. Parks steered the car down an exit ramp and headed east, closing the distance between them and the cozy modern retirement center where he knew his mother would be eagerly awaiting their arrival.

"Hello, hello!" Grandma Parks called from across the small neatly appointed room as the group appeared at the open doorway. "Come on in and make yourselves comfortable. It's so good to see you. And this must be Olena. Oh, you are such a lovely girl!"

The young Russian smiled shyly, immediately drawn to the kind eyes and warm manner of the woman seated by the window. She followed Tony and Tie Li to the wheelchair and extended her hand. "How are you, Mrs. Parks?" she said politely.

"A handshake? From a family member?" The woman waved her hands. "Why, my dear, we give hugs around here. Now you just bend down a little so I can give you a good squeeze."

Olena complied and found herself engulfed in a firm

loving embrace. The old woman's thick white hair smelled fresh and clean, just like the room.

"Tony has told me so much about you," Grandmother Parks announced, motioning toward a little computer resting by the bed. "He says you're staying with them in Chicago until your mother returns. He also said you've been helping him with an experiment of some sort."

"That's right," Olena nodded. Raising a suspicious eyebrow, the girl glanced over at Tony, then asked, "And what else has your grandson said about me?"

The old woman grinned. "Oh, this and that." She winked at her grandson. "He did mention something about a keyboard."

Olena grew embarrassed. "I'm, uh, sort of glad he caught me," she admitted. "If he hadn't, I'd be living in the shelter or shipped off to some state institution somewhere. The Parks' apartment is a *lot* better—and safer."

Tie Li pressed close to her grandmother. "Olena and I have a great time together. She's smart, sorta like Tony, except she knows regular stuff."

"What's that supposed to mean?" Tony asked with a frown.

"She knows about things *other* than computers," the girl stated.

Tony thought for a minute. "Oh, yeah. I guess she does."

Grandma Parks grinned broadly, driving wrinkles from her face as she basked in the joy such visits brought. For the next hour the family members exchanged the latest news about uncles, aunts, and cousins as well as a litany of aches and pains each was being forced to endure. Tie Li explained in great detail her recent escapades at school and how she scored second in math class, beat out by a boy who she figured had a computer for a brain. "Kinda like Tony only with dark hair," she suggested.

At one point Olena quietly slipped, unseen, out of the room. A certain sadness had wrapped itself around her heart. She didn't have a family anymore. She had no mother or grandmother to whom she could tell her tales.

With a deep sigh Olena sat down on a bench in the brightly-lit hallway. Oh, how she missed her family and having a home of their own!

"You sound sad," a breathy, wavering voice called through a darkened doorway nearby. Olena wasn't sure if the comment was directed at her.

"Why?" the unseen speaker asked. "Is someone sick today?"

The girl stood and peered into the shadows. "Are you talking to me?" she asked.

"You aren't from this country, are you?" came the quick reply from the darkness.

"No, my mother and I are Russian."

"Russian? How wonderful! I hear Russia is very beautiful."

There was a pause. Then Olena heard the mysterious speaker clear her throat, a process that sounded painful. "Please, come in. I'd like to talk with you."

Olena glanced down the hallway toward Grandma Parks' room. She could hear Tie Li's happy laughter mingling with the soft cadence of TV sets entertaining the occupants of several apartments nearby. Slipping into the chamber, she glanced about. "Why isn't there any light in here?" she asked, while waiting for her eyes to adjust to the darkness. Thick curtains covered the window, and she noticed that there were no lamps resting on any of the small tables looming in the shadows.

"I don't need any light," the unseen resident announced. "Haven't for years."

As she grew more accustomed to her surroundings, Olena noticed the frail outline of a woman seated in a wooden rocking chair. Dim slivers of light squeezing past the drawn curtains revealed bony hands folded in a small lap, and narrow shoulders hiding behind the worn pattern of an old silk dress. Above the shadow-masked face she could just make out a faint tangle of unruly gray hair held in place by a hand-sewn cap. A white cane leaned against one arm of the chair.

"Oh," Olena said softly, "you're blind."

The old woman laughed. "Only in my eyes," she stated. "The rest of me sees quite well."

Olena tilted her head slightly. "What do you mean?"

"Well," the woman said after clearing her throat once more, "I know that you're not very tall, and you're young; 14, 15 years old perhaps. You're wearing walking shoes. And since you don't swish when you move, you've probably taken off your coat. How am I doing?"

The girl chuckled. "Good!"

"I also know that you're very sad. I heard you sigh in the hallway. That's not the sound of a happy teenager."

Olena settled at the end of the carefully made single bed. "I don't want to bore you with my problems."

"It's all right," the old woman encouraged. "I want to know. Really."

With that she leaned forward, moving her body into the dim light. Suddenly Olena's breath caught in her throat. The woman's face was twisted and scarred, her eyes hidden under dark layers of uneven tissue that long ago had sealed off her sight forever.

Olena gripped the side of the bed with all her might, turning her knuckles white. She wanted to scream, to gasp, to run. The old woman's face was so disfigured and repulsive, so frightening, that the girl found she couldn't breathe. She could only sit and stare at the horrible sight, unable to speak, to move, to think.

"Please," the woman's bent and swollen lips invited, "please tell me why you're so sad." Before Olena could answer, the woman went on, giving her visitor another moment to adjust to the trauma of the moment. "I know what it's like to be sad," the old woman said, her voice rough and strained. "Heaven knows I've had my own share of pain."

Slowly the face retreated back into the shadows, allowing the darkness to hide it from view. "I lost my little girl, my precious little girl, and my husband in a fire many, many years ago. I tried to save them, but . . . I couldn't. I was badly burned. The last thing I ever saw was a wall of flame falling toward me. The doctors said I was lucky to be alive." Her voice faltered. "But God is good, and I praise Him every day for His blessings."

Olena frowned, trying to regain control of her racing heart. "God?"

"Certainly," the old woman said with conviction. "Without God, there's nothing in this world worth living for."

"B-but you lost your sight and everything!"

"Not everything. I didn't lose God. He's with me even in the sad times, when my heart feels like breaking and I don't think I can stand another day. Why, just this morning I asked Him to bring me a friend, someone to talk to, maybe even someone I could help or encourage. Then I heard you sigh out in the hallway. I like to believe that God answered my prayer."

The girl closed her eyes, trying to shut the image of the face from her thoughts. "My sadness isn't like yours," she said.

"It doesn't matter," the old woman responded.

Olena shook her head. "How can you love a God that allows horrible things to happen? How?"

The woman leaned forward again, bringing her face back into the dim sliver of light filtering through the thick curtains. Olena refused to divert her gaze, staring instead at the rough folds of skin covering the area where eyes should be. "When I was a child, my father would take me to the big stone church near our apartment in the city. The pastors were so kind and gentle. They would tell stories to us children, stories from the Bible.

"One man, Pastor Richard, told us the story of Daniel in the lions' den. It frightened me, so he took me on his knee and told me something I've never forgotten. He said, 'Rebecca, Daniel loved God so much that he was willing to die for Him. That's why he wasn't afraid of the terrible beasts in the den.'" The woman paused. "Don't you see? If you're not afraid of dying for God, that makes living for Him possible. It doesn't matter what lions you face, whether it's a fire, or loss of a loved one, or even having to live in a world of darkness, because God is there. He's always there."

Olena allowed her gaze to drop to the folded hands in the woman's lap. "Tell me," she said softly. "How do you find this God?"

The old woman's lips formed a crooked smile. "Don't worry," she said. "He'll find you."

Muted laughter echoed from the hallway as Tie Li and the others left Grandma Parks' room. Olena smiled in the darkness. "Thank you," she said. "Thank you for talking to me."

"Wait," the old woman called as the girl stood. "You still haven't told me why you're sad."

Olena thought for a minute. "If I write you a letter, is there someone here who can read it to you?"

"Yes," her companion responded with a twisted grin. "My nurse. She reads the paper to me every morning after breakfast."

"Then I'll write to you," Olena said. "You'll soon be getting a very long letter from me."

"Oh, that would be wonderful!" came the enthusiastic reply. "I like letters, especially from friends."

At the doorway the girl paused. "I just remembered something. I don't know your whole name."

"Rebecca. Just send your letter to Rebecca. They'll know who I am."

"All right, Rebecca. I'm Olena. I hope your nurse can read my not-so-wonderful handwriting. I tend to scribble."

"You should see my handwriting," the woman sighed.

Olena chuckled, then her face relaxed into a soft smile. "Goodbye, Rebecca," she called into the shadows.

From deep in the darkness a voice responded. "Goodbye, Olena."

Tony scratched his head and wrinkled his nose. "This is weird," he said.

Tie Li and Olena looked up from a fashion catalog. "What's weird?" they asked.

The boy pointed at his computer screen. "SIMON says they lived *under* some mountains."

"Who?"

"The Waldenses."

"Who?"

"The Waldenses, the people in our next simulation."

Tie Li turned to her friend. "Well, we've been on top of some mountains with my silly brother. Guess now we're going under some."

The older girl stood and walked across the vacant space of the empty thirty-sixth floor of Mr. Parks' office building. "These Waldenses, did they have to fight the beast too?"

"Well, they didn't come right out and tell everyone what they believed about the Bible and the Creation Sabbath and stuff like that. They were kinda secretive."

"What do you mean?"

Tony typed a command on his keyboard and then stood back from the wall. "We'll find out soon enough." Lifting the device to his lips, he ordered, "SIMON, begin simulation A44, full effects and power."

Tie Li stood quickly to her feet as the wooden bench on which she'd been sitting transformed itself into a solid boulder. The walls and wide ceiling forming the vacant office complex suddenly became rough stone embankments, complete with dripping water and frozen-in-time stalactites. Darkness swept over the area, save for a single oil lamp burning somewhere down a narrow passageway off to the right.

To complete the simulation, Tony's powerful computers projected random walls of stone reaching from the floor to the ceiling, creating a mosaic of small rooms and alleys, each bathed in shadows and wrapped in cool moist air.

"Wow," the boy gasped, glancing at his surroundings, "SIMON wasn't kidding when it said some of the Waldenses lived *under* a mountain."

"Where are we?" Olena asked, bending low to move to where Tony was standing.

"In the Italian Alps, along the border with France. It's about the middle of the fourteenth century. The printout from SIMON's search says the religious powers in Rome were very strong then. Anyone who didn't go along with their ideas and practices, anyone who didn't worship on the first day of the week and openly defile the seventh, were finding themselves very dead."

Tie Li joined the two by the jagged wall. "So these Waldenses, they're hiding in here?"

"Usually they were out among the mountains planting crops and minding their own business, but SIMON reports that sometimes soldiers from Rome would wander through the mountains, taking prisoners or killing these 'enemies' of Rome."

A rustle echoed from a nearby passageway, causing the trio to turn suddenly. They saw a young boy, probably no older than 5 years old, stumbling along the rock-strewn alley, a wrapped parcel held tightly in his chubby arms.

Reaching an intersection, he paused and listened. From somewhere deep in the cave came a soft scratching, as if someone was rubbing a fingernail over a piece of wood. Tie Li and the others saw the boy smile, then head in the direction of the sound.

"Come on," Tony ordered. "Let's follow him."

CHAPTER 10

GOING UNDERGROUND

The little boy seemed to move with purpose, ignoring the fact that he was alone in the mighty Alps, the range of towering mountains separating France from Italy. He moved in the shadows like a phantom, his sandaled feet shuffling over the stone floor of the dimly lit cave.

Every once in a while, he'd stop and listen. Tony, Tie Li, and Olena listened as well. Yes, the sound was still there, a soft scratching noise being generated in some distant corner of the labyrinth. The determined lad would hurry on, drawing ever closer to the source of the mysterious disturbance.

Finally, he emerged into a rough-walled room surrounded by shadowy stone barriers boasting dripping rivulets of water. At the far end of the small expanse rested a wooden table and bench, where a man sat hunched over a parchment. A hawk quill waved before his face as he wrote.

"Daddy!" the boy called out, running the final few yards across the chamber. "I found you all by myself!"

The gentleman laid down the writing tool and welcomed

his son with open arms. "Yes, you did. I'm very proud of you too. You're a fast learner, my son. You can find your way in any cave, I'm sure."

"I just followed the sound of that," the child announced, pointing at the quill. "It went scratch, scratch, scratch, and I came."

The man hugged his son warmly. "What a beautiful lesson you just taught me," he said. "You see, I'm preparing another copy of the Bible for others to read. If they follow the writing, just as you followed the scratching, they'll find their Heavenly Father, only this Daddy won't be human like me. And He won't be hiding in a cave."

"He won't?" the boy asked.

"No. He'll be sitting on clouds of glory, coming to redeem His people from all the ages, just like this Book has promised."

"I know the Bible," the little boy stated, wiggling down from his father's lap. "Listen."

The child planted his feet firmly on the stony ground, lifted his right hand, index finger extended, and called out in a firm, well-rehearsed tone, "Remember the Sabbath day by keeping it holy. Six days you shall labor and do all your work, but the seventh day is a Sabbath to the Lord your God. On it, you shall not do any work." The miniature preacher smiled. "That's Exodus chapter 20, verses eight, nine, and 10. How did I do?"

"Fine, fine!" the man exclaimed, clapping his hands together in fatherly glee. "Why, you'll be the best preacher in all the mountains of France. Italy, too. But," the speaker's voice turned somber, "you can't say those words to just anyone. Only those who truly want to know the Lord. Even then you must speak quietly and with great care. There are those who don't want to hear words from the Bible. They'll hurt you if you don't speak just the way they want you to speak and believe as they believe."

"I know," the little boy replied. "I'll always be careful, father."

"Good. Now, I wonder what's in that package you carried with you through the cave. Could it be some of your mother's fresh made bread and cheese?"

"Apples, too," the child encouraged. "She said you'd be as hungry as a bear."

"And I am. As a matter of fact, I think I'll just eat you up with my dinner!"

The boy squealed in delight as his father jumped up and began chasing him around the dark confines of the subterranean chamber. Nearby, smiles lit the faces of Tony and the others.

"It isn't dead, is it?" Tie Li said.

"No," Tony agreed. "The truth is still alive, although for a long time its champions had to live in caves and hidden valleys. Rome had a hard time finding them. For 1,000 years, the Waldenses sent out missionaries who sometimes passed themselves off as peddlers, handing out handwritten bits and pieces of the Bible along with jewelry and silks. Those that got caught preaching Bible truth were tortured and killed. It was terrible. But in the mountains they were usually safe."

Tie Li shook her head. "I think it would be just awful to know that, at any moment, someone might kill you because of what you believe."

Olena turned slowly. "No. No, it's not."

Tony blinked. "You know about this?"

"Not me," the girl said softly. "Someone I met recently. She said if you are willing to die for God, then it is possible to live for Him, too, even when you're in pain or suffering a great loss. Now I know what she meant. The people in these caves had already decided that they were willing to be killed instead of change what they believed. It was more important to them than to be alive." Olena looked about at the damp walls. "That's how they could stay in caves and hide in mountain valleys for so long. They believed in something. They believed in the truth."

Tony nodded slowly. "Kinda gives you, I don't know, hope?"

"Hey," Tie Li asserted, "I think we've found the two best beast killers."

"What?"

"Truth and hope! It's a great combination even here under the mountains."

Tony glanced at the electronic device in his hands. "At least we found what one of those Beings meant when it talked to John the Revelator on the Island of Patmos. You know, about not worshiping the beast. I guess if you have the truth backed up by a bunch of hope, you can beat the beast at its own game." Lifting the metal box to his lips, Tony called out, "SIMON, end simulation."

The cave walls and passageways vanished, leaving the three young people standing at the center of the empty office complex. "But," Tony continued, "there were two other announcements by two other beings that day, remember?"

"Yes," Olena said thoughtfully, "something about Babylon and . . . a judgment from God. What did those things mean?"

Tony lifted his hands. "OK, OK, I'll get on it. But for now, we'd better head home before our dad sends out the FBI to find us. It's almost eight o'clock. If we're not in our rooms in 30 minutes acting like dedicated students, he'll get fidgety. You guys head on out, and I'll catch up after I shut everything down. And don't drink all the grape juice in the refrigerator. Mom bought that especially for me."

"Sure," Tie Li called over her shoulder as she and Olena headed for the elevator, "we'll save some for you. You want one drop or two?"

"Hey! That's *my* grape juice," Tony whined. "Why don't you two drink something else?"

Olena smiled and winked over at her young companion. "I don't know. I'm in a grape juice mood—how about you?"

Tie Li nodded. "I've been thinking Welch's all afternoon."

Tony sighed. With any luck at all, he'd get half a glass of his favorite fruit drink. Perhaps he should have told them that he was thirsty for orange juice.

As he was about to shut down the final system, he noticed that the mailbox symbol was flashing on one corner of the main screen, indicating that yet another message was waiting for him to download off the company's e-mail system. Tony grinned and reached for his device. "OK, Dark Angel," the boy breathed, "you want to talk to me. Then go right ahead. This time I'm going to answer you—with a vengeance."

The words scrolled onto the screen in glowing letters. "Those people were fighting a losing battle," the message stated. "So are you." As before, the reply indicator blinked yellow, revealing that the writer was still online waiting for a live response.

Tony did nothing. He just sat stone still, watching the small illuminated panel next to his elbow flash numbers in a blindingly fast sequence.

"Good never wins. Evil rules!" The words danced across the monitor, enticing the boy to action. But he remained motionless, staring at the device.

"Why aren't you responding?" the unknown writer queried.

A smile began to lift the corners of Tony's lips as, one by one, a column of numbers stabilized on the little device's display. *25-93-A, 25-93-B, 25-93-C.* Tony watched with growing excitement. "Come on, SIMON," he urged quietly, "Do it. *Do it!*"

25-93-D, 25-93-E . . . Cross-check: finalizing.
Firewall: penetrated.
Line monitoring: locked.
Virus insertion: standing by.
Remote computer location: determined.
Waiting for backlash command: [press F5].

Tony rushed to the main keyboard and quickly typed, "Hey, Dark Angel, compute this!" Then he slammed his finger down on the F5 key.

The large monitor glowing brightly in front of his face flashed off and then on again as total system power was transferred to one single action. The words Tony had typed were wrapped in an electronic packet and sent, at the speed of light, out of the building, traveling in the blink of an eye to the destination SIMON had determined was the source of the incoming message. Attached to the five-word sentence was a powerful virus created with one goal in mind: to disable Dark Angel's modem permanently.

The boy watched as the next message began to scroll. You can't touch me. I sf9ol;ls. .sf..a**8%^%$^68-0 . . .

"Yes!" Tony shouted, punching the air with his fist. "Yes!" Pointing at the now blank mailbox he added, "Two can play at this game. You fry me. I fry *you!*"

As suddenly as the glee had rushed over him, a feeling of sadness flowed into the young boy's thoughts. He'd just done something he'd never done before. With his carefully crafted virus, he'd destroyed a functioning piece of computer equipment. But more importantly, he'd shut down a communication link with someone who obviously didn't believe in the God for whom he and his adopted sister had been searching. In their journeys they'd found a Jesus who'd accepted abuse without insisting on revenge. They'd discovered a certain hope based, not on destruction, but on life and new beginnings.

Tony slumped onto a stool and stared at the blank screen for a long moment. In the stillness of the empty thirty-sixth floor, perched high in the towering office building, Tony spoke softly into the cool, still air. "What have I done?" he whispered.

"Here it is," Tie Li called from her comfortable spot by the window. Afternoon rays filtered through the lacy curtains and imprinted their delicate designs on the rug at her feet.

Olena looked up from her biology assignment. "Here what is?" she asked.

"Babylon. It's a city."

"Where?"

"In Iraq."

The older girl drummed her fingers on her book. "Didn't America fight a war over there once?" she asked.

"In Babylon?"

"No. Iraq."

"Oh, yeah," Tie Li said. "I remember seeing some of it on TV." The girl shuddered, then continued. "Now, let's see, what was the capital of Iraq?"

Olena lifted her textbook. "I'm studying biology, not geography. I have enough trouble figuring out what city I'm in."

"Chicago."

"Chicago is the capital of Iraq?"

"No! You *live* in Chicago."

"I thought you were looking for Babylon."

"I am."

"So, what are you doing in Chicago?"

"Aaahhh!" Tie Li put her hands over her head as if trying

to keep it from exploding. "You're confusing me." She bent low over the atlas and scanned the colorful images spread across the pages. Then she turned to the index and brightened when she saw a familiar word. "OK. Now, listen," she instructed. "Babylon is an ancient city located near Baghdad in the country of Iraq. Got that?"

"Got it."

"Because of its location at the main overland trade route between the Persian Gulf and the Mediterranean Sea, it prospered for many centuries until Xerxes the First destroyed it while trying to quell a local revolt. The temples, towers, and statues were reduced to rubble." The reader looked up. "That was in 482 B.C."

Olena shrugged. "I wasn't born yet."

"Of course you weren't born yet. Neither was anyone else who's alive today, including Grandma Parks, and that's saying a lot."

The older girl nodded thoughtfully.

"Anyway," Tie Li continued, "the hanging gardens of Nebuch . . . Nebuch . . . Nebuchadnezzar were considered one of the Seven Wonders of the Ancient World."

Olena frowned. "Didn't one of those Beings in Tony's simulation say that the city had fallen down or something?"

Tie Li nodded thoughtfully. "These modern-day pictures of Babylon prove that's exactly what happened! There's nothing left but ruins and a bunch of tourists wearing fanny packs and huge hats."

A soft bump at the door interrupted the girls' conversation. "Who's there?" Tie Li called.

"It's me, Tony."

"Tony who?"

There was a pause. "Tony, your brother, who, if you don't open the door, is about to drop three cups of hot chocolate all over the hallway."

Olena jumped to her feet. "Hot chocolate? Come in. Come in!"

Tony stumbled into the room, balancing cups and saucers in his outstretched hands. Thin, vaporous wisps of steam rose from each as the two girls guided their visitor to the study table at the end of the bed. "I don't do this for just anyone, you know," Tony stated, trying to sound official. "But since you're all part of my virtual reality experiment, I thought I'd reward you for your hard work and willingness to get blown up if something went wrong."

"Blown up?" Olena gasped. "No one said anything about getting blown up!"

Tie Li shook her head. "Oh, don't listen to him. He's just trying to make us think he's super smart and that our lives are in his hands."

Tony glanced at his sister. "Is it working?"

"No."

"I didn't think so."

Olena sipped the sweet liquid and closed her eyes in delight. "This is good, Tony. Thanks for thinking of us."

"Well, I wanted to talk to you about our next sim, you know, give you some background information and stuff."

Tie Li lifted her hand. "Wait a minute, All-Glorious Computer Head. Can you explain something to me?"

Tony poured the hot chocolate that had spilled over into the saucer back into his cup. "Shoot, All-Weird Sister."

The girl grinned, then pointed at the book lying open on her bed. "It shows in there that Babylon is nothing but a pile of ruins in Iraq. Why did the Being announce something that wasn't even a secret? I mean, anybody can see that the city is gone. What's the big deal?"

Tony savored his rich chocolate drink as he thought for a minute. "When the Being said those things to John the Revelator, John understood something about the city's history that you don't know, or that book might not say."

"Such as?"

"According to the data SIMON collected from the historical archives in Jerusalem—they have a web page and everything—Babylon used to be a successful trading center on the River Euphrates. But, it was also something else, something very disturbing. Both the Being and John understood that fact."

Olena blew cooling air over her cup. "Understood what?"

Tony looked first at one girl and then another. "At one time, for God's people, Babylon was a prison."

CHAPTER 11

DIGGING IN WITH DR. ABBOTT

ootsteps echoed down the long, tiled hall as Tony, Tie
Li, and Olena made their way past solemn-faced statues and colorful mosaics depicting forgotten battles.
Winged beasts and spear-wielding warriors etched on
stone panels provided a somber glimpse into ancient history. Glass-covered showcases sheltered shimmering arm
bracelets, golden chalices, and decaying weapons of war.

Finally, the three visitors arrived at a large wooden
door guarded by a rubber tree plant and a sign that read,
"Dr. Nathaniel Abbott, Director, Chicago Institute of
Antiquities." Tony knocked softly.

"It's open," someone called from behind the door.

The trio entered a large room decorated with similar
but smaller relics. Sagging bookshelves bowed under the
weight of thick volumes and piles of file folders. A computer hummed softly atop a paper-littered desk by a tall
window. Seated in a sturdy leather chair, a bearded man
was holding what looked like two small horses held apart
by a metal shaft. "It's a bronze bit," he announced proudly.

"A *what?*" Tony asked, edging closer to the desk.

"A bit. You know, for putting in a horse's mouth so you can steer it. Look at these cheek-pieces. What detail! What craftsmanship! Made in about 900 BC in the Zagros Mountains of Iran. Interesting people. Supplied Assyrian armies with battle animals and—" he held up the relic, "—and bits." The man gently lowered the ancient item to his desk, then looked at Tony. "Who are you?"

The boy cleared his throat. "I'm Tony Parks and this is my sister, Tie Li. Olena here is our friend."

"I see. Well now, have you seen our museum?" the man asked.

"No, sir. We just arrived. I called you—"

"Not much interest in antiquities nowadays," the man interrupted. "People would rather watch a video or go to a theme park. I don't really blame them. Ancient relics don't do anything. They just sit on a shelf and look old. Why are you here?"

The boy blinked. "I, uh, we called and asked about Babylon and—"

"Babylon. Beautiful city. Good work being done there. They've uncovered so much. Did you know that Babylon had walls 80 feet thick? Imagine that! And 300 feet high, too. They didn't have hydraulic cranes or dump trucks. No cement mixers. Just people power. And good architects. Wonderful designers, too. Yes, they had to be very gifted. So, how may I help you?"

Tony shook his head. Keeping up with Dr. Abbott was proving to be a challenge. "Sir, we'd like some information on the city of Babylon and how it relates to the Old Testament story of the Jews, God's chosen people."

Dr. Abbott sat up a little straighter in his chair as a smile peeked from behind his graying beard. "My, my. You sound like you've done some research on the subject."

"Yes, sir. I checked out your computer records and—"

"Computer records? Our network isn't open to the public."

"Oh, yes sir, I know. That's why I only scanned your index and didn't download any information."

The man's eyes opened wide.

Tony continued. "I read an article you wrote recently in a magazine about how the city fell to Cyrus the Great in 539 BC when his Persian invaders diverted the river that ran under the walls, letting them sneak in at night and take control of the city and—"

"You were interested in my article?" the man said in apparent surprise. "At your age?"

Tony nodded vigorously.

Dr. Abbott smiled. "Good for you! Funny you should mention the Euphrates incident. That little piece of Jewish history isn't usually talked about outside of historical circles. But, where are my manners? Please, everyone, be seated."

Tony, Tie Li, and Olena glanced about the room. Every chair was stacked with books, papers, or yet-to-be-catalogued relics. "We'll just stand," Tie Li announced with a grin.

The man nodded, leaned back in his chair, and began waving his finger in the air as he drew an imaginary map. "Now, let's say here's Babylon, a great and powerful kingdom run by Nebuchadnezzar—you know, the fellow who built the hanging gardens?" The three visitors nodded in unison. "And over here are the kingdoms of Israel and Judah, the divided, so-called 'Promised Land' of the Jews. Well, King Nebbie decides that the Jews possess some valuable real estate—their country is on the main overland trade route between Europe and Africa. So the monarch summons his generals. 'Take your armies and make those Jews an offer they can't refuse,' he tells them.

"Well, being good Jews and not wanting to give up their Promised Land, the Hebrews fight back—poorly. Most of them are exiled to Babylon.

"Over time, they get comfortable in their new location. They farm, start businesses, make money, and basically live a good life."

"Wait a minute," Olena interrupted. "I thought you said they were *exiled* to Babylon. Doesn't that make them prisoners and the city their jail?"

"Yes. But not all prisons are nasty places filled with nasty people. Babylon was rich, overflowing with successful people who enjoyed culture and the finer things in life. I guess you could say that the city proved to be a 'gilded cage' for the exiled Jews. Many of them adopted the local religions, most of which were based on idol worship. They didn't even want to go back to what was left of their old 'Promised Land.'"

Tony leaned forward slightly. "So you're saying that the Jews, God's chosen people, *liked* being in Babylon?"

"That's what I'm saying," Dr. Abbott responded matter-of-factly. "Oh, there were a few, such as Daniel and others, who recognized that their nation was being destroyed by prosperity and idol worship. The Jewish people as a whole were beginning to ignore the God of their forefathers. Their children weren't being taught the old ways. Their nation was simply falling apart in a land that rejected anything related to the God of Heaven."

Tie Li frowned. "So, what happened?"

"After Babylon fell to Cyrus, he allowed those few who wanted to return to Jerusalem to do so. He even helped them rebuild their temple. You might be interested to know that over a hundred years before Cyrus was born, the prophet Isaiah predicted all this would happen. He even called Cyrus by *name!*

"Jerusalem eventually regained its former glory, complete with newly constructed walls and a beautiful place of worship. But for generations after that, children heard the story of the Babylonian captivity and how a nation almost lost sight of their God while living in the dangerous lap of luxury."

Tony nodded slowly. "So, when the Being on Patmos shouted, 'Babylon is fallen,' John the Revelator understood that he was really saying, 'Don't become too comfortable in a world of sin, even if it feels good and makes you think you're safe, because you're really in a kind of prison. Right?"

Dr. Abbott blinked. "How do you know these things, young man? You're just a boy."

Tony smiled respectfully. "Yes, sir. But I want to know the truth. We all do. I believe in God and Jesus, even though it's sometimes hard to figure out what's going on in the Bible. So I use my computer and smart people like you to explain things to me."

"Well," the curator said, "you're on the right track. Most Christian theologians agree that Babylon also meant any power that forced people to disobey God. That would be a form of spiritual imprisonment, wouldn't it? I suggest you learn what another Being said later in John's book. This one told everyone to 'come out' of Babylon. You might want to think about that too."

Tony smiled. "Yeah. Hey, thanks, Dr. Abbott. That's all we wanted to know."

The man stood and gripped the boy's palm in a firm handshake. "My pleasure," he said. "Good luck on your search."

With a wave, the three young visitors exited the room, leaving the museum curator alone among the relics of the past.

"So," Tie Li said as the three young people stepped out of the elevator high atop Mr. Parks' Chicago office building, "we've decided that *coming out* of Babylon doesn't mean leaving a *place* called Babylon. It means getting away from anything that doesn't preach, teach, or believe Bible truth. That I understand. But, what is Babylon *today?* We're not prisoners like the Children of Israel were. We can choose to believe anything we want. Right?"

Tony walked over to the main computer terminal. "That's right, little sister. But . . ." he typed a command, "remember why we're doing these simulations? Remember why I created SIMON in the first place?"

"Yes. You wanted to find out if what Jesus said was true; His promises, the New Earth, stuff like that."

Olena shook her head. "That's why *I'm* here. I want to believe there's something better coming in the future."

Tony turned to face the girls. "I'm trying to find out those things too. But isn't it good enough that Jesus said it? I mean, why don't we trust Him?"

Tie Li thought for a long moment, then her mouth dropped open. "Wait a minute. That's it. That's *it!*"

"What's *it?*" Olena asked.

"Don't you see? We don't trust Jesus. We don't really believe what He said because we're *prisoners!*"

"Prisoners?" the older girl scoffed. "We're not prisoners."

"Yes, we are," Tony interjected, nodding at his sister as his own thoughts connected with hers. "We're prisoners of the lies Satan has been telling everyone for 6,000 years. He persuaded generations of so-called religious people to hide the truth. He's made us think that just maybe what Jesus said isn't true. So we doubt and want to have everything proven to us.

"We're prisoners, all right, and so are many others. And lots of them don't really seem to care. They just go to church or watch TV or shop at the mall and don't even worry about what's right and what's wrong. They let other people do their thinking for them."

The boy shook his head. "But not us! We're not going to stay prisoners any longer. This is one Babylon we're getting out of right now!"

Olena grinned. "Tony Parks, you're a regular John Wesley."

The boy stopped typing and stared at his companion. Tie Li's eyebrows rose, wrinkling her forehead. "What did you say?"

"I said Tony was like John Wesley."

The teenager chuckled. "How do you know about John Wesley?"

Olena lifted her hands and said, "You're not the only truth tracker around here. I did some reading last night about the Reformation in Europe, about how men such as Wycliffe, Jerome, and Huss did things like translate the Bible into everyday language so everyone could read it. They also told people about the lies the church in Rome had been spreading." Olena sighed sadly. "Of course, many of those preachers were burned at the stake, but not before they made a lot of people start thinking for themselves."

The girl walked to the center of the large expanse as Tony and Tie Li following in amazed silence. "Did you know that the religious powers of that time were so mad at Wycliffe that 40 years after he died, they dug up his bones and burned them just to prove that they were right and He was wrong? *They burned a dead man's bones!*"

Tony shook his head. "It took SIMON hours to compile information on the Reformation," he said. "And you found this just by reading something? Where? What?"

Olena giggled. "You left your computer on when you went shopping with your folks last night, so I put the encyclopedia disk in the CD."

"By yourself? I thought you didn't know anything about computers."

"I don't. I just did what I've seen you do, you know, click on the little pictures? Well, when I did, it asked me what I wanted to know. So I typed in Bible and preacher, and there it was."

Tony's grin spread wide. "Well, you're about to learn more about John Wesley. He's in my simulation for today."

Tie Li looked over at her friend. "This is scary," she whispered. "You're turning into my brother."

The older girl laughed. "No," she said under her breath so only Tie Li could hear, "I just read one section of the report. I didn't want our favorite genius to think he's the only person on earth who knows how to find out things."

After Tony finished entering a set of instructions at his terminal, he called over to the girls. "Hope you don't mind crowds."

"Crowds?" Olena responded. "I thought we were going to see John Wesley?"

Tony nodded. "We are."

Lifting the device to his lips, the boy ordered, "SIMON, begin simulation A45, full effects and power."

In a flash, the empty floor of the office building became a stone-paved city street teaming with people. Tie Li and Olena watched as children raced by, following a distant voice shouting into the cool, damp air.

"England," Tony announced, answering the girl's unspoken question. "1700s. Wesley's preaching is stirring things up. Let's listen."

Above the din of the crowd, a strong male voice grew louder and louder. The man stood in a small city park, surrounded by leafy trees and a canopy of cloudless sky. Above the sea of heads and shoulders, Tony, Tie Li, and Olena could just make out the eager face of a young preacher as he waved his arms and pointed at the towering arches of stone churches rising beyond the gathering.

"I'm telling you the truth," the voice shouted. "The Kingdom of God is not confined to a church, it is *within you!* It's in your heart. You can speak *directly* with the Master of the universe!

"They tell you that you must live a certain way, pay certain indulgences, and depend on holy men for forgiveness from sins. But I tell you that we're *all* sinners, and we always will be. The *only* way to reach heaven is through Jesus Christ. It's His righteousness that makes the difference, and not our deeds. Our best works do not impress God. If we *do* achieve some degree of goodness in our lives, it is because Jesus is living within us. By ourselves, we can do nothing. But with Jesus, we can do all things."

Tony glanced at Tie Li and Olena, then fixed his eyes once again on the preacher.

"It's Jesus who forgives," the man said with great earnestness. "Jesus who saves, Jesus who sets our course for glory. Like the angels that appeared to John the Revelator, I say to you, Babylon is fallen. *Come out of her, my people!* Leave the confusion and lies. Leave the comfortable path that leads to destruction. Take the hand of Jesus in yours, and don't look back until you've reached the Promised Land to come."

The crowd roared in response, filling the air with their happy voices. But in the midst of the joyous occasion, Tony and the others saw Wesley suddenly slump back into the arms of some supporters. A hush fell over the gathering as strong hands carried the moaning preacher through the throng. Blood could be seen streaming out of a deep gash in the man's head, staining his white shirt.

"What happened?" Olena gasped. "Tony, what happened?"

"He'll be OK," the boy whispered. "Seems not every-one appreciated what he was saying. Whoever threw that stone must like things the way they are. I guess you could say that he or she was perfectly happy to live in Babylon."

At Tony's command to SIMON, the scene was gone, leaving the three young people standing in the empty office complex.

The boy shook his head. "The Bible never said that coming out of Babylon was going to be easy. It just says it will be worth it in the end."

Tie Li sighed. "Did a lot of people listen to those preachers and Bible translators?" she asked.

"Yes, but not enough of them. SIMON's research found that God had to do something dramatic to catch the attention of the next generation."

"Really?"

Tony pointed toward the ceiling. "Believe it or not, 100 years after John Wesley preached in England, a strange thing happened in America."

"What?"

The boy smiled. "The sky fell."

CHAPTER 12

FAMILY MATTERS

Tony cradled the phone at his ear and waited. On the line he could hear a familiar chortle, indicating that another phone was ringing at some distant location.

"Hello?" a quiet voice answered.

"Hey, Mr. Lester. This is Tony. I'm here at work, and you're not. Are you sick or something?"

"No," the unseen speaker responded. "I've just got some family matters to attend to."

"Family matters?" Tony chuckled. "I thought you didn't have a family."

There was a pause. "Well, something came up. I won't be in today . . . or tomorrow either."

The caller frowned, sensing that all wasn't well with his boss. "Mr. Lester, is there anything I can do to help?"

"Nah. You just stay at work and do the normal maintenance routines on 23. Finance needs a new CD-ROM, and marketing has been hounding me to get the latest version of PC-TrackIt installed on their network server. Don't forget to have someone sign the licensing agreements."

Tony nodded as he scribbled notes on a small pad by

the telephone. "Don't worry, boss, I've got it covered," he encouraged, then paused. "Are you sure everything's OK? You sound kinda down."

"Don't concern yourself. Just do your work and try not to destroy anything else in the process."

The boy's eyes narrowed. "Anything *else?* Hey. I take good care of company equipment. You said so yourself."

"Yeah, I did, didn't I? Stay out of trouble, Tony, and I'll be in touch tomorrow."

"You can e-mail me," Tony suggested. "I'll check my box when I get in after scho–."

"No!" Mr. Lester interrupted abruptly. "I'll call you." He softened. "We'll just use the telephone like normal people. OK? See ya, Tony."

The line went dead as the speaker hung up.

Strange, Tony thought to himself. *What's with Mr. Lester? He's not his usual weird self. Must have the flu or something. And what's with this family business? I thought he lived alone.*

The boy shrugged. There was no time to worry. He had lots to do before supper. Besides, tonight was going to be special. He and the girls would witness a simulation that would blow their minds. Even now, SIMON was hard at work gathering data and preparing to recreate a scene right out of history and Bible prophecy. Yes, it should be quite a show.

Olena sat at a window on the far side of the empty office space, gazing down at the city. Cars moved slowly, heading south and west, leaving the towering buildings and glass-fronted apartment complexes behind.

The people on the streets looked like ants trudging through some gigantic maze, their thick dark coats and covered heads making them seem even less human. In the distance, the snow-covered plains rolled to the horizon, their surface hidden under a tattered blanket of snow.

"Do you know what I wish?" Tie Li heard her say.

"What?"

"I wish I could do anything I wished for just one hour."

"Why?"

Olena pointed at the streets. "Then I'd go down there and make everyone happy. I'd give them lots of money. If anybody had cancer or some awful disease, I'd zap it right out of their bodies. Then I'd build everybody a big house to live in, with big windows and a huge backyard filled with apple trees and strawberry patches." She paused. "Oh, and all the families would be together, you know, with a mother and father and brothers and sisters. There'd be no police cars, no guns, no drugs—just people going around being nice to each other. That's what I would do."

Tie Li joined her friend at the window. "Well, *I'd* make sure that nobody ever fought wars, and all bombs in the whole world would be thrown into the ocean where the salt water would turn them into mud."

The girl glanced over at her brother. "How 'bout you, Tony? What would you do if you could do anything?"

The boy looked up from his keyboard. "I'd give everyone a computer."

Tie Li and Olena glanced at each other. "Figures," they

said in unison.

"Hey, that's not a bad thing," Tony countered. "With computers, you can find out information and make better decisions. You can create more powerful medicines and learn how to save the rain forest. Think about it. Computers can do almost everything."

"Oh, yeah?" Olena challenged. "They can't bring us hot chocolate on a cold winter evening."

Tony's face flushed crimson as he waved his arms. "OK, computers can't do everything. I know one thing for sure: they couldn't cause the event we're about to see. I've programmed SIMON to replicate a portion of New England in the mid-1800s. We're going to a small farm in upstate New York near the Vermont border. There's a guy there that some writers and historians say started a revolution among Christians of his time. He went around telling people that Jesus was getting ready to return to earth. He based his reasoning on Bible prophecy. You wanna check it out?"

"Let's do it!" came the enthusiastic reply.

"SIMON," Tony ordered into his device, "begin simulation A46, full effects and power."

The empty office complex went dark. Then, slowly, the skeletal outlines of trees and the rough faces of granite rocks began to form about them. Wind moaned in the brittle grasses, sending virtual leaves tumbling past their feet. Overhead the sky hung silent, spreading a vast canopy of stars from horizon to horizon.

The shadowy presence of a large, wooden barn loomed nearby, and beyond it, nestled near a grove of trees, a farmhouse sat bathed in dim starlight. Somewhere far away, a dog barked.

"Oh," Tony said suddenly. "I was supposed to read something to you first."

"What?" Tie Li asked.

The boy fished a piece of paper from his jacket pocket and unfolded it.

"SIMON found this in the Bible, in Matthew. It says that one day Jesus was telling His disciples about what it would be like near the end of the world. You know, right before He came back." Tony squinted to see the words. "It says, 'Immediately after the tribulation of those days shall the sun be darkened, and the moon shall not give her light, and . . .'" the boy glanced up at his companions then back at the paper, "'. . . and the stars shall fall from heaven.' Neat, huh?"

Tie Li looked up into the night sky. "I don't see anything happening."

Tony lifted his wristwatch close to his face and pressed the illuminator button. "Wait for it," he said. "It'll happen at 2 a.m." He hesitated, then glanced skyward. "And that's right about now."

A single shooting star arched across the sky, leaving a thin trail in the inky blackness of space.

"That's it? That's all?" Olena chuckled.

"Not exactly," Tony said, looking toward the east.

The two girls turned to face each other. "I don't see anything," Tie Li announced.

At that moment, Tony's watch chimed the two o'clock hour. "Get ready," he said. "Here it comes."

Tony, Tie Li, and Olena waited, eyes searching the vast darkness overhead. The stillness of night wrapped them in cold arms, driving shivers deep into their bodies. Would it happen just as Jesus said? Or was the Bible simply a collection of fairy tales and hopeful guesses?

Suddenly, the entire universe seemed to explode. The three fell back in mute amazement as the sky filled with sparkling streaks of light arching across the emptiness of space, creating dazzling, multicolored bursts, blistering trails, and trembling ribbons of fire. The blasts all seemed to be coming from a common point in the sky, setting off fingers of vapor and burning gases that spread with unthinkable speed to the north and south, east and west.

Not one portion of the charcoal canopy escaped the rush of color and brilliance. The trees that had moments before been shadowy sentinels in the darkness now stood out in stark relief, their naked branches reflecting the silver, yellow, and orange luminescence flashing overhead.

Tie Li was about to speak when the door of the distant farmhouse burst open and a man wearing a woolen bathrobe and slippers ran across the yard, a woman close at his heels.

"Look!" he shouted, dancing in the starlight pulsating over the farm. "Just look, Lucy! Do you see it? *Do you see it?*"

"Well, of course I do," the woman announced, gazing skyward while trying to keep her husband within arm's reach. "I do believe the whole sky is tumbling right down on our farm!"

"Here and there and *everywhere!*" the man shouted. "Jesus said it would happen. John the Revelator did too. Remember?" He lifted his hands as if he were preaching to a great throng. "The stars of heaven fell unto the earth, even as a fig tree casteth her untimely figs, when she is shaken of a mighty wind." Well, my dear, God's shakin' that fig tree tonight. He's just a-shakin' it with all His might."

"Now, William, don't get so excited."

"What do you mean, 'Don't get so excited?' This is a direct fulfillment of Bible prophecy! Jesus said it would happen, and here it is, right over our heads. Praise God. *Praise God!"*

The man ran to his wife and grabbed her hands. "Lucy, I'm right. My calculations are correct. This is the beginning of the end. Prophecy points to this event, this time in history. Now I know for certain. Jesus is coming soon. *He's coming soon!* The very sky is announcing it. First was the dark day 63 years ago. About the same time, the moon turned the color of blood. And tonight the stars are falling. They're falling, Lucy, because Jesus said they would!

"Don't you see? *God is faithful.* He's faithful! Just as the prophets foretold the rise and fall of governments, of civilizations, of earthly powers, the Bible said that one night, right before Jesus came back again, the stars would fall from the sky. Well, look up, Lucy. See them fall? It's begun. The time of the end has begun!"

Suddenly another figure burst from the grove nearby. A man ran through the eerie glow, stumbling along, unable to take his eyes from the sky. "Pastor Miller? *Pastor Miller?"* the new arrival shouted. "It's the judgment, isn't it? God is judging us and will destroy us all this very night! Oh, what should we do? I don't want to die!"

"No, Brother Reed," the farmer called back, "it's not a sign of judgment, but a sign of hope. The stars are telling us that Jesus will come just as He promised."

"But I'm afraid," the visitor moaned. "Before Jesus returns He has to judge us. Am I ready? I don't know. I just don't know!"

With that the man ran back toward the grove, his body straining under a load of anguish and uncertainty. Overhead the meteor shower continued, illuminating the barn, the house, and the upturned faces of William Miller and his wife, Lucy.

"SIMON," Tony said quietly into the device. "End simulation and play back audio of last statement of man from grove."

As the scene slowly faded away, a recorder by the wall repeated the man's urgent cry. "But I'm afraid. Before Jesus returns, He has to judge us. Am I ready? I don't know. I just don't know!"

Then all was quiet.

Olena lifted her hand. "The first Being," she said softly. "It said something about God judging the earth, didn't it?"

Tony nodded and spoke into the device. "SIMON, play back message of the first Being on Patmos stored in simulation A41."

The young people heard a computer's hard drive chirp, then a powerful voice filled the empty space of the office building. "Love God. Glorify Him because He has come to judge the earth. Worship Him who made everything!"

Tie Li frowned. "So, the man from the trees was right? We'll be judged before we can go to heaven?"

"I guess," Tony agreed.

"Then I may as well give up hope right now," Olena

sighed, a frustrated tone in her voice. "I'm not exactly what you'd call a saint. Your God will not let me into heaven."

"Me neither," Tie Li joined in. "I'm always doing stuff I shouldn't, like getting mad at someone at school or saying things that hurt people."

Tony nodded slowly. "I know what you mean. I'm afraid I'm a poor choice, too." The boy glanced at his sister, and then at Olena. "I'm sorry, guys. I guess I set us all up for a big disappointment. If God is going to judge us, and we're all bad, we're not going to live in heaven . . . ever. I'm . . . I'm sorry."

Three sad, despondent young people left the empty thirty-sixth floor of the office building that night. Their hopes had been dashed, crushed under the weight of their own imperfections. Olena's heart was breaking. Heaven and a New Earth had been her only hope. Now the future seemed dark and lonely once again, not only for her, but for her mother as well.

That night, Tony couldn't sleep. He kept replaying in his mind the images of the men and women who'd appeared in SIMON's simulations: the apostle Paul, John the Revelator, Columba of Iona, the Waldenses, John Wesley, William Miller and his wife Lucy. All of these people had lived with the hope of heaven and a New Earth to come. Didn't they know about the judgment? Didn't they realize how sinful they really were even though they did good deeds and helped people? Those were just outward things.

But inside, where evil lurked, they were human, and that meant they were sinful.

Tony slipped out of bed and walked to his desk. It wasn't fair. It just wasn't fair. History was filled with brave people who lived and died for God. But no one was sinless as Jesus had been. And since heaven would be filled with those God judged as worthy, there wouldn't be anyone to greet the Saviour when He returned.

The boy sighed a long, aching sigh. There had to be an answer somewhere. He must've missed it, overlooked it, bypassed it in his search of the past.

Tony strolled across the bedroom and switched on his computer. Maybe, just maybe, there was still hope to be found.

CHAPTER 13

(HAMPION)
OF TRUTH

elf-test messages flashed across the screen. In the mid-night stillness of his room, Tony loaded SIMON into the machine's powerful memory. At the ready prompt, he picked up the device and spoke. "SIMON," he said, "scan all versions of the Bible and find the answers to the following questions."

"SIMON standing by," his metallic partner responded.

Tony ran his fingers through his hair as he formulated the right words to say. At last he spoke.

"SIMON, what is the condition of all people before the end-time judgment?"

The computer was silent for a minute. The boy knew that a great flood of information was being processed, Bible chapters and verses compared, meanings deciphered, by the logical electronic brain hidden in his computer. Soon the result of SIMON's search flashed onto the screen. In glowing yellow letters the word *SINNER* pierced the darkness.

Tony sighed. Now for the hard one. "SIMON," he said, "what is the condition of all people *after* the end-time judgment?" The boy waited, almost afraid of what he would discover at the end of SIMON's investigation. The world had been filled with sin and sinners ever since Adam and Eve had turned their backs on God's law of love. Would anyone escape the beast? Would anyone be successful in his or her attempt to come out of Babylon?

SIMON churned through the information stored in its mammoth hard drives and in the neatly stacked collections of memory chips. As always, Tony's application was extremely thorough, leaving no recorded thought, statement, promise, or prophecy untouched by its probing investigation. There was absolutely no room for error in the answer; no second-guessing or half-baked theories would be allowed. SIMON would accept none of these emotional elements that are so common to human thought. Its answer would be based on fact, not fiction. Reality, not tradition.

At last the examination was complete. SIMON flashed its one-word answer on the screen. Tony's eyes opened wide as a look of amazement spread slowly across his face. "Are you certain?" he gasped.

"Yes," SIMON responded.

There, floating in a sea of electrons, bathed in its own light, was the answer. Brilliant yellow letters formed the word *FORGIVEN*.

Tony felt excitement begin to build deep in his chest. "How?" he gasped. "SIMON, how is it possible?"

This time the answer was almost immediate. Without hesitation the name *JESUS* appeared on the screen.

Tie Li was returning from the bathroom when Tony burst into the hallway. She jumped in fright. "What's the matter with you?" she gasped, gripping her bathrobe and trying to regain her breath.

"We're going!" Tony almost shouted.

"Going where?"

"I've gotta tell Olena," the boy said. He raced in the direction of Tie Li's room, his sister trying to keep up.

"She's asleep!" Tie Li whispered hoarsely as the two stumbled through the doorway.

Tony ignored her warning. "Olena! Olena! We can go. It's OK! We can live in the new earth!"

The Russian girl opened one eye and then quickly pulled the covers up to her chin. "Tony Parks, what's the matter with you? And why are you dancing around like this in the middle of the night?"

"Don't you know what this means?" her unexpected visitor cried, his words tumbling over themselves. "You can have your bay window and big yard with lots of apple trees and strawberry patches. You and your mom can live together forever where there's no sickness or death or people stealing things from you. It's OK. We're forgiven. *We're forgiven!*"

"What do you mean?" Tie Li asked.

Tony sat down at the end of Olena's bed, then stood up again, unable to sit still. "Jesus forgives," he stated excitedly. "He's forgiven everyone. It's the second step. Don't you see? The Beings said it to John on the island. First you're judged, but because Jesus died for sinners, you're judged as savable. You're forgiven! Then you're supposed to leave your sinful life behind—you know, get out of Babylon. Then you fight against anything that tells lies about God. That's the beast. You fight the beast because it doesn't preach the truth. One, two, three. Judged, forgiven, fight for truth. It's so logical. So simple!"

Tie Li frowned. "You mean everybody's saved? Even child molesters and bank robbers?"

Tony shook his head. "No. That wouldn't make any sense. Those people would hate heaven. They couldn't hurt kids or steal stuff 'cause heaven isn't like earth. But they can choose to be saved if they want to be. All they've got to do is ask God to help them change."

"How?"

The boy thought for a minute. "Remember what John Wycliffe said to the people in England before someone struck him with a rock? He said God's kingdom is inside us. Inside us. It's our choice. We can either choose to be forgiven or refuse to be forgiven. So going to heaven is something we decide. And after we make that choice, we change—you know, get out of Babylon, fight the beast, stuff like that."

"I get it," Olena nodded. "You're saying that Jesus forgives us, but we have to accept it or it doesn't do us any good."

Tony smiled. "Exactly. It really makes sense, doesn't it?"

"Yeah," Tie Li stated. "That's what all those people you've been showing us were saying. They were telling people to believe in the truth, to believe in Jesus, because that's the only way they could get to heaven."

The girl thought for a moment as she listened to a siren wailing in the distance. "Tony?" she said. "All these champions of truth . . . they lived so long ago. Are there any left today? Is there anybody out there telling people about what the Bible really says?"

Tony shook his head. "I don't know, Tie Li," he said soberly. "They were all from history. Who are the champions of truth today?"

Olena laid her head against her pillow and closed her eyes. That was a good question. Who would tell her mother about the new earth to come? Who would tell her there was hope beyond that cold jail cell in Texas with the iron bars and peeling paint? All the apostle Johns and Columbas and Waldenses and Wycliffes and Millers were dead and gone. All the faithful men and women who'd stood firm in their faith had vanished like clouds after a storm. Were there none left to tell the world what was really true about God and heaven and the future?

Suddenly, a thought sprang into her mind, a thought so fantastic, so incredible, that she refused it at first. But it pressed in anyway, filling her body with an exciting, almost breathless exhilaration. She looked up at her friends, a smile lighting her young face. "I know who the champions are today," she said quietly.

"You do?" Tony asked.

"Yes," Olena responded. "We are. We can be today's champions of truth."

Tony and Tie Li looked at each other, then back at Olena. Could it be? Was it possible? Did they dare believe that they could join the likes of the Reformers, Bible writers, and Christian pioneers in telling the world about the beast and Babylon and the sin-shattering promise of forgiveness?

The announcement blaring from the loudspeaker echoed throughout the bus terminal. "Attention, all passengers. Greyhound's Heartland Express is ready for boarding at gate 5. Please have your tickets in hand to show the driver. All aboard!"

"That's me," Olena said, gathering her few belongings and standing to her feet. "Austin, here I come."

"Olena," Mrs. Parks said warmly, "I'm so glad Social Services has arranged for you to be near your mother."

"As soon as she is released, you two can begin a new life together," added Mr. Parks.

Olena nodded, trying her best to hold back tears. "I'll miss you guys," she said softly.

Tie Li wrapped her arms around her friend. "You will always be my sister, even if you live in Texas."

"I know," the girl said, shaking her head. "I know."

Turning to Tony, she held out her hand. "Thank you," she whispered. "Thank you for teaching me so much about the past—and the future."

Tony's smile trembled just a little. "You're welcome, Olena."

The girl bent forward and planted a shy kiss on the boy's cheek, then hurried away. "Goodbye," she called over her shoulder, not looking back. "Goodbye."

Tony and Tie Li were quiet as the Parks family drove back toward the heart of the city. They were several blocks from the apartment building when Tony asked his father to stop the car. "I need to check and see if there's any work for me," he declared. "I'll be home in time for supper."

"OK, honey," Mrs. Parks responded as the vehicle

paused at the curb. "I'm making soup and sandwiches. Don't be late."

"I won't," the boy called as he hurried across the sidewalk.

Entering an apartment building, Tony hurried to the address registry posted on the wall. Scanning the titles, he smiled when he noticed a familiar name. Checking the information against a letter and number scribbled on a piece of paper in his pocket, he bounded up the steps and finally stood outside apartment 4-G. Straightening his shoulders, he rang the bell and waited.

Before long the door opened the length of its chain lock. "Tony Parks, is that you?"

Tony smiled sheepishly. "Yeah, it's me. May I come in?"

The door closed, then opened wider. "Why?"

The boy grinned. "Is it a crime to visit your boss on his day off?"

Mr. Lester shook his head. "I . . . I wasn't expecting visitors."

"I'm not a visitor. I'm your fellow nerd. Remember?"

The man sighed. "Well, as long as you're here, you might as well come in."

Tony smiled and entered the small apartment. Afternoon sunlight filtered through the curtains, highlighting the dust particles hanging in the dry air.

"Nice place," Tony said, glancing around. "Who's your housekeeper? Hurricane Andrew?"

Mr. Lester chuckled. "Not exactly."

At that moment a child who appeared to be about 5 years old stumbled into the room. The girl worked hard to keep her balance above two metal braces lashed to her legs. She propelled herself forward by leaning heavily on crutches extending from her elbows to the floor.

"Hi," she called out, a little out of breath. "I'm Anne Marie. Who are you?"

Tony's brow furrowed slightly. "I'm . . . I'm Tony."

"Hello, Tony," the girl said with a smile. "That's my Uncle Jerry. Do you know him? He's nice. He takes care of me when my daddy is gone on a trip. I've got a dog named Doolie and a fish that eats worms. Well, I gotta go take my nap now, because Uncle Jerry said if I don't I won't get to watch cartoons. See ya, Tony."

With that the child hobbled back down the short hallway and disappeared through an open door. Mr. Lester glanced at his visitor. "She, uh, I take care of her when my brother travels out of town. She's been sick, so I'm kinda staying home to make sure she gets her medicines. Can't always trust baby-sitters, you know. They're too busy watching music videos or running up my phone bill while talking to boyfriends in South America or some other expensive place." The man paused. "Why are you here?"

Tony looked down at his feet, then back up at his boss. "Mr. Lester, I had SIMON, my computer program, trace a message I sent a few days ago to someone called Dark Angel. I . . . I think I kinda knocked him out of business." The boy paused. "You'll never guess what address it listed."

The man turned slowly and walked into the kitchen as Tony followed. On the table, spread out in tangled, ash-stained piles, were the remains of a computer.

Tony gasped, then moaned, "Oh, no! I didn't know it would do this much damage!"

"That was some virus," Mr. Lester stated, eyeing the darkened mess. "I had a firewall installed and everything. Your code bypassed it like it wasn't even there and put the main processor into a self-generating loop, causing an uncontrolled surge in the power supply. Before I could get to the plug, the whole thing sparked out. Scared Anne Marie half to death. I ended up dumping orange juice all over it trying to stop the meltdown."

Tony's hands shook as he picked up the scorched remnants of a high-speed modem. "Oh, Mr. Lester. I'm . . . I'm so sorry. Really. I know what this computer meant to you."

"Hey," the man said, "it's just a bunch of transistors trying to think like a human. I'll start saving for another one."

"Why?" Tony pressed. "Why did you write those things to me?"

Mr. Lester shook his head. "You and your big ideas," he said, a touch of anger in his voice. "You think you can solve all the world's problems with a computer, with logic? That's not what the world is like, Tony. It's filled with sick children and lonely apartment buildings. You have no idea what people are going through. You don't know how it feels to watch someone you love screaming in pain as doctors try to straighten bent legs and deformed bones. It hurts, Tony. It hurts you so deep inside that it makes you mad. You want to scream too. You want to reach out and strike the world on the face and say, 'Leave me alone.' But you can't. You have to stand there and take it, day after day, year after year. You have to stand there alone because nothing can help you—no person, no computer, nothing."

Tony closed his eyes as sudden tears ached for release. "Mr. Lester, you're wrong. You're not alone. I know that now."

"Yeah? Who's with me? Huh? God? Look around, boy genius. Do you see God in this apartment?"

Tony shook his head. "You can't see Him, You . . . you gotta feel Him. And if you can't feel Him, you just gotta know that He's there because He promised. You see, Mr. Lester, Satan's been telling you lies. He's been saying that there's no hope, that we're alone in this world. But there *is* hope; there's hope for today and for the future."

The man slumped to a chair and buried his face in his hands. "You're talking nonsense, Tony Parks."

"No! I'm telling the truth," the boy insisted, moving closer to his boss. "I want to tell you a story, Mr. Lester," he said, "a story about how God and the devil fought a war and we got caught right in the middle of it. You see, there was this garden . . ."

The late-afternoon sun hung low over Chicago as a bus headed south out of the city. Above a drab street a boy poured out his heart to a man in a cluttered downtown apartment while powerful computers sat silent in the empty thirty-sixth floor of an office building. There would be no more simulations, no more journeys into the past. The machines had done their work and done it well. Now it was time for lives to be touched and hope reborn in those fortunate enough to come face-to-face with a new generation of champions of truth.

THE END